ON THE FUGITIVES' TRAIL

Wolf Bixler—Raised among Comanches, feared and hated by whites, he was a notorious gun-tough who'd kill a man as soon as look at him. A fortune in gold awaited him, if he could live to collect it.

Stu Jarrell—A respected U.S. Marshal, he wanted Bixler behind bars. But if he was to survive the deadly trail to San Antonio, he would have to trust the outlaw with his life.

Rosa—In the first flush of womanhood, she found herself torn between two gringos—the idealistic lawman and the cynical hard case.

Armand—Rosa's younger brother, he had left safety and luxury behind and now faced a world of betrayal and danger, a proving ground for manhood.

Pedro—The guide who would get them through, he played a dangerous game. If he outwitted his enemies, he'd still have to deal with his friends.

The Stagecoach Series
Ask your bookseller for the books you have missed

STAGECOACH STATION 25:
SAN ANTONIO

Hank Mitchum

Created by the producers of
Wagons West, White Indian,
and **Saga of the Southwest.**

Chairman of the Board: Lyle Kenyon Engel

BANTAM BOOKS
TORONTO · NEW YORK · LONDON · SYDNEY · AUCKLAND

STAGECOACH STATION 25: SAN ANTONIO
A Bantam Book / published by arrangement with
Book Creations, Inc.

Bantam edition / September 1986

Produced by Book Creations, Inc.
Chairman of the Board: Lyle Kenyon Engel

ISBN 0-553-26180-0

Published simultaneously in the United States and Canada

PRINTED IN THE UNITED STATES OF AMERICA

O   0 9 8 7 6 5 4 3 2 1

STAGECOACH STATION 25:

SAN ANTONIO

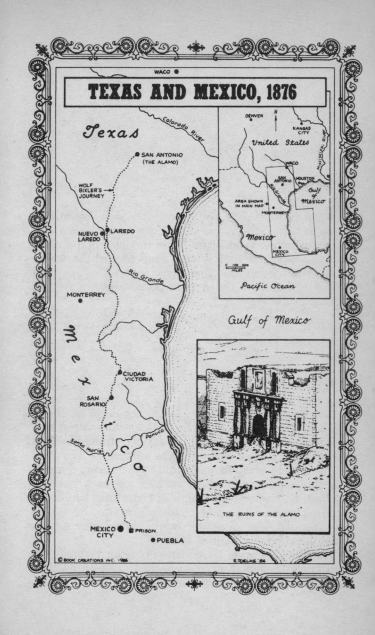

TEXAS AND MEXICO, 1876

WACO

Texas

Colorado River

SAN ANTONIO
(THE ALAMO)

WOLF
BIXLER'S
JOURNEY

NUEVO
LAREDO — LAREDO

Rio Grande

MONTERREY

M
e
x
i
c
o

CIUDAD
VICTORIA

SAN
ROSARIO

Panuco

Santa Maria

MEXICO • ☐ PRISON
CITY
• PUEBLA

Gulf of Mexico

DENVER   N
                        KANSAS
                        CITY
United States
              WACO

              SAN
              ANTONIO   HOUSTON
AREA SHOWN
IN MAIN MAP   Gulf
                      of
              MONTERREY Mexico

Mexico

MEXICO
CITY

0 100 300
    MILES

Pacific Ocean

THE RUINS OF THE ALAMO

© BOOK CREATIONS INC. 1986   R. TOELKE '86

Chapter One

A gusty wind, raw with November's chill, whistled through the cracks in the shutter covering the narrow, barred window. Wolf Bixler lay in the back of the dark, solitary cell, his sleepless eyes fixed toward the sound of the wind. Soon the same cracks that let in the wind would reveal dawn's gray light, heralding the start of his last day on earth.

He decided that the cold air in the cell was not so much from the icy wind, but more from the sinister presence of Death, almost tangible in the room. Death and Wolf Bixler had been face to face many times during the forty years of his violent life.

"You've come too close to getting me, old boy," he murmured. Rubbing his shirt, he thought of the three different times lead slugs had been dug out of his chest. With rough fingertips, he traced the white-ridged scar that ran from the corner of his right eye straight back to where the top of his right ear was missing.

Abruptly he was aware of a dull light filtering through the shuttered window. He rubbed his eyes wearily, rattling the twelve-inch length of chain that bound his wrists together. Rising to a sitting position, he swung his shackled legs over the bunk's edge, placing his booted feet on the wooden floor.

Watching the gray illumination coming through the thin cracks in the shutter, he sighed. "Well, old boy, looks like this is your day to win. November twenty-first, eighteen hundred and seventy-six. You knew it all along, didn't you? You *always* end up winnin' sooner or later. Ain't nobody gets away from you."

Wolf lifted his two hundred and sixty pounds off the bunk and stood full height, six-feet-six in bare feet. He made an enormous shadow in the small cell as he spoke to Death again. "I ain't eager to fall into your clutches, old fella. But if you're gonna look for me to grovel just before you take me, you can forget it. Wolf Bixler don't crawl and whine for nobody."

Moving slowly with the weighty leg irons, the condemned man shuffled to the window and swung open the shutter. The air was cold on his scarred, bearded face as he peered through the bars into the gathering light. He could make out the uneven rooflines of Mexico City in the distance and towering mountain peaks beyond.

Looking closer at the open area inside the prison walls, Wolf focused on the framework of the ten-foot-high gallows, and a sick chill swept over him. The swaying noose was silhouetted in the gray morning light.

Suddenly he heard voices, and six men appeared in the courtyard. Five were prison guards, dressed in drab, olive-colored uniforms. The sixth was José Villa, the prison's hangman, a dark little man the color of smoked leather. Dressed in solid black, Villa was carrying on a conversation with one of the guards, apart from the others. They talked for several minutes while the other men lit cigarettes and talked in Spanish.

Wolf Bixler watched as Villa stepped to the gallows and took hold of the lever that worked the trapdoor. Twice he jerked the lever while the guards looked on casually, but the trapdoor did not fall. Villa swore and jerked it again. This time, after a two-second delay, the trapdoor sprang downward with a hollow clatter.

Villa told the guard close to him, whom he called Pedro, to put the trapdoor back in place. Pedro crawled through the framework and snapped it upward.

Once more the hangman pulled the lever, but the door remained in place. Cursing, Villa pulled the lever

hard, and again after a two-second delay, the trap flew
open. Wolf heard Villa tell Pedro to fix it immediately.
It had to be ready in an hour.

Wolf lifted his eyes toward the eastern sky, now
turning pink—the last sunrise he would ever see.
Strange, he thought, how good the world looks when
you're about to leave it.

His attention was drawn to the cluster of guards, who
burst into laughter. Apparently one of them was telling
a joke. They were quiet for a moment and then broke
into laughter again. Wolf watched them with cold black
eyes. How could they be so nonchalant when they were
about to watch a fellow human being die?

Or are they human? he asked himself. *Maybe the
only real humans are Indian.*

The condemned man's mind raced back over the
years to his first childhood recollections, vague and
sketchy memories of life in a Comanche village somewhere in west Texas. The Comanche chief, Wounded
Hawk, and his squaw, Red Fawn, were childless and
had taken him into their home as their son.

Wounded Hawk had told the little white boy the
story many times. A Comanche war party had found
him wandering alone on the plains, a dirty, hungry,
frightened child no more than five years old. They
brought him to the village, and Red Fawn quickly grew
attached to him, teaching him the language of the
Comanches. He had never learned who his real parents
were or what had happened to them.

His Indian parents had given him no name until as a
young lad he found a wolf pup whose mother had died.
He adopted the pup and raised it with tender care and
love. Wounded Hawk and Red Fawn had named him
Little Wolf because of it.

The condemned man watched the eastern sky turn
orange as he remembered how within a year the wolf
pup had grown into maturity and run away. Little Wolf
was heartbroken and pined for his furry pet, but the
animal never returned.

As Little Wolf grew into manhood, his white skin
became an issue with some of the young Comanche

braves. They were learning to hate white men and were being trained to kill them. Yet here was a white man living in their midst.

Little Wolf soon realized he no longer belonged with the Indians. In many ways he thought like them, but he could not pretend to be one. He was a white man, though he had developed the taciturn manner characteristic of the Indians.

He decided he must go. Wounded Hawk and Red Fawn did not want their adopted son to leave, but they accepted his decision.

The day he left the village, the aging Comanche chief looked at his adopted son, who towered over him, and said, "Little Wolf will return to us from time to time, will he not?"

The twenty-one-year-old man, now wearing the clothes of the white world, turned from the tear-stained face of Red Fawn and replied, "Yes, my father. I will visit you."

Wounded Hawk knew he must not let his tumultuous emotions show. It was beneath the dignity of a Comanche chief to do so. "There is one thing you must do, my son," he said. "Since you are going to live in the white man's world, you must have a white man's name."

"I had not thought of it, Father. What name shall I use?"

The old man rubbed his chin for a moment, looking at the ground reflectively. Then lifting his gaze to Little Wolf's face, he said, "The white trader who comes here and who helped you remember the white man's tongue— he has been friend to Comanche. His name is Albert Bixler. Let your name be Albert Bixler."

Little Wolf looked at his adopted mother, who was wiping tears from her eyes, and then turned his coal-black eyes back to Wounded Hawk. "Though I must go and live with my own people," he said softly, "I cannot leave everything of my Comanche life behind. You have named me Little Wolf. I will keep part of it forever. My name will be Wolf Bixler."

A smile tugged at the corners of Wounded Hawk's wrinkled mouth. "Then so it shall be." He nodded.

After embracing the elderly couple, the tall white man had mounted his horse and ridden away.

Wolf Bixler's mind was snapped back to the present by the pounding of a hammer. He saw that the guard assigned to repair the faulty trapdoor in the gallows was underneath the platform, working furiously.

Shafts of sunlight were spreading across the sky from the earth's eastern edge in changing sheets of color. He could hear the ever-present rats scratching in one of the dark corners.

He let his thoughts drift back again. From the Comanche reservation, he had ridden eastward to Abilene, Texas, where he had learned that a nearby rancher was looking for a man to break horses. Wolf had broken horses for the Comanches since he was in his early teens, and he considered himself qualified for the job.

Riding through the gate of the Diamond T Ranch, Wolf dismounted at the back porch of the large house. An elderly woman was busy tending two small children, and she looked up as Wolf approached.

"Afternoon, ma'am," he said, touching his hat brim. "I understand the owner of this place is lookin' for a man to break horses."

"Why, yes," she said, seeming a bit awed by his size. "That would be my husband, Walt Tomberlin. You will find him over there by the barn."

Wolf thanked the rancher's wife and led his horse to the huge barn. After tying the animal near the corral gate, he entered the barn, immediately struck by the smell of the old hay, leather, grain, and horse manure. He heard voices near one of the stalls at the back.

Wolf stepped close and saw three men looking at a cut on a bay mare's flank.

"Excuse me," he said in his deep bass voice. "I'm lookin' for Mr. Tomberlin."

"I'm Tomberlin," answered the oldest of the three as he rose to his full height of six feet. He was slender and narrow-shouldered, with a silver mustache that matched the hair on his head, mostly covered by a broad-brimmed Stetson. "What can I do for you?"

"My name is Bixler, Mr. Tomberlin. A man in town said you were lookin' for a fella to break horses."

Squinting at the giant, Tomberlin said. "You have experience?"

"Yes, sir."

"Where you from?"

"West Texas."

"*This* is west Texas. I mean who have you broken horses for?"

Wolf knew if he told the rancher that his total experience was breaking Indian horses, he might not get the job. "Ranchers all over," he replied. "Names don't stick with me."

Sizing up the big man, Tomberlin said, "You look like you could handle the job. I'll let you take a crack at it. If you're good, you're hired. I've got two dozen that need breaking right now. I'll pay you ten dollars a head."

"I can do it," Wolf said with confidence.

"Hey, boss," spoke up one of the other men. "Why don't you let him try breakin' Diablo?"

Arching his eyebrows, Tomberlin said, "*Diablo?*"

"Sure!"

"Aw, now, Archie," the rancher said wryly, "this man wants to live to break more horses."

"What is Diablo?" Wolf queried.

"Meanest animal this side of hell," Walt Tomberlin responded. "You don't want to mess with him. Nobody can break Diablo. I just keep him around as a conversation piece."

"I'd like to try," said Wolf.

The rancher laughed. "Tell you what, Bixler. You earn your two hundred and forty dollars breaking those two dozen horses, and if you've got any rump left, I'll give you a shot at Diablo. You break him, I'll pay you a hundred dollars!"

"Good," Wolf replied. "I'll break Diablo *first*."

"You won't be alive to ride the others," the third man cynically commented.

Wolf Bixler had broken many wild Appaloosas and there wasn't a meaner horse on earth than an Appaloosa that had made up its mind no human was going to stay on its back. "I can break him, Mr. Tomberlin," he said firmly.

The two cowhands looked at each other with sly grins.

"Let him try it, boss," Archie urged. "What have you got to lose? You were lookin' for a bronc buster when this guy showed up."

"All right," said the silver-haired rancher, shaking his head. "You two get Diablo in the corral and put a saddle on him. Better have a couple others help you."

Wolf and the rancher walked out beside the corral. Word spread quickly that some new fool was going to attempt to ride Diablo, and men were gathering along the fence, hoping to glimpse the horse's new victim. When they saw him talking with Walt Tomberlin, several comments were made about Wolf's size.

Suddenly a gate was opened on the far side of the corral, and a herd of two dozen horses thundered through in a cloud of dust. Among the animals, Wolf saw a huge black-spotted stallion that moved like it was king of the corral. It laid back its ears and snapped at one horse with its teeth, then shouldered another aside as it pranced proudly among the herd.

"That must be Diablo," Wolf observed, and Tomberlin nodded.

Archie and three other cowhands moved among the herd with lariats, but Diablo, eyes bulging, kept other horses between itself and the men with the ropes. Little by little, the four men worked it apart and looped their nooses over its head. While they held it with their lariats wound around a husky pole near the center of the corral, another cowhand put a bridle on Diablo, forcing the steel bit between its teeth.

The big animal was breathing heavily, its nostrils flaring. It flinched as another man slipped the saddle blanket over its broad back. A cowhand carrying a saddle walked past Tomberlin, and Wolf said, "Let me put that on him, friend."

Saddle in hand, Wolf crawled through the fence poles and strode toward the huge animal. Diablo crouched on its haunches as Wolf threw the saddle on its back. Tossing the left stirrup over the saddle seat, he drew up the front cinch and tightened it. Diablo shifted, drew in a long, deep breath, and held it.

Wolf gritted his teeth and said, "Think you can outsmart me, eh?" He gave the cinch a powerful yank, and the huge animal released the indrawn breath. It came through the flared nostrils in a whistle.

Wolf fastened the hind cinch loosely, dropped the left stirrup, and took hold of the reins with his left hand. Swinging into the saddle, he said, "Okay, boys, take your ropes off."

The instant the horse's head was free, it hunched and snorted. The cowhands dashed for the fence as the angry animal bounded across the corral, its big frame arching against the unwanted weight on its back. Lunging, lurching, and bucking, the devil horse was determined to dislodge Wolf Bixler.

The Diamond T cowboys watched in awe as Wolf stayed in the saddle despite the pounding Diablo was giving him. His hat sailed off his head while the world whirled around him with the constant surging of the horse's powerful muscles. Dust clouds rose as the savage animal plunged its head between its front legs and repeatedly kicked its heels in the air. Each time it hit the ground, it expelled a loud scream and then violently shook its massive frame and rose again.

A cheer went up around the corral as man and beast battled for supremacy. Wolf's left arm felt as if it would pull from its socket with each lunge, but sheer grit and determination held him on Diablo's back.

The horse varied its course across the corral, twisting and arching its back, but Wolf Bixler was like a cocklebur in sheep's wool, and he clung tight.

Diablo soon seemed to realize it was not going to buck this man off. In a wild frenzy, it laid back its ears, rolled its eyes, and lunged for the pole in the middle of the corral. Wolf understood that the vicious animal intended to push its side against the pole and crush its rider's leg, so he pulled his foot from the stirrup and raised his leg high—just as Diablo slammed against the pole.

He almost lost his balance before he could get his foot back in the stirrup, but he managed to hold on. Next the horse tried scraping him against the corral fence, but again it failed to dislodge him.

Snorting in fury and pounding the earth with its mighty hooves, Diablo made a final effort. Dipping its head, the horse went into a somersault, intending to crush the man in the saddle as he came down hard on his back. Wolf had been through this with the wicked Appaloosas, and when he saw it coming, he leaped from the saddle.

The huge horse rolled over, breathing heavily, and rose to its feet. Just as it was gaining its balance, Wolf vaulted back into the saddle, jerked the animal's head sideways with the reins, and gripped the mane with his other hand. "Okay, boy," he breathed, "I'm ready for more. Let's go."

To Wolf's surprise, Diablo relaxed and settled down. Releasing his grip on the mane, he gave the horse its head, and Diablo, docile as an old workhorse, trotted around the corral. The onlooking crowd of ranch hands threw their hats in the air and cheered the stranger.

After walking Diablo around the corral several times, Wolf guided the horse to the spot where Walt Tomberlin stood and swung from the saddle. "There you are, Mr. Tomberlin," he panted. "Anyone can ride him now."

Tomberlin smiled. "Looks like I owe you a hundred dollars. I'll write you a check, and you can take the rest of the day off."

Wiping sweat, Wolf accepted his hat from a cowboy who had retrieved it, and said, "Did take the steam out of me. I'll ride into town and get a room at the hotel. Tomorrow I'll start on the other horses."

"You won't have to stay at the hotel while you're breaking broncs for me." Tomberlin smiled. "You can stay right here in the bunkhouse." Pulling out his checkbook, he produced a pencil stub and asked, "What's your first name, Bixler?"

"Wolf," replied the big man.

"Wolf?" The rancher's eyes were skeptical.

"Yes, sir. I was raised by Chief Wounded Hawk of the Comanche tribe. He named me Wolf."

Walt Tomberlin looked as if he had just smelled sour milk. His voice sailed across the warm afternoon air. "You were raised by stinking, scaly-bellied *Comanches*?"

Wolf's jaw muscles stiffened and corded when he saw several men whirl around at the rancher's shrill words. "You are speaking of my people," he said. His piercing eyes glinted with hostility.

Tomberlin's men drew near. One of them yelled, "Hey, boss! Don't tell me we've got a dirty Indian lover here."

Wolf turned to scowl at the man.

In a grating tone, Tomberlin rasped, "No Indian-loving white turncoat works for me!" He slipped his checkbook back into his shirt pocket and then, narrowing his eyes into mere slits, said icily, "Get off my land."

Wolf Bixler was getting his first taste of white men's contempt toward Indians and anyone who befriended them. His eyes filled with smoldering rage and he hissed, "I broke that horse for you. I ain't leavin' without my hundred dollars."

"That's what you think!" Tomberlin snapped. "Get on your horse and ride."

Wild fury ripped through Wolf. Ejecting a deep growl like that of a giant grizzly, he lunged for the impudent rancher, his powerful hands gripping Tomberlin's narrow shoulders. "I want the money I earned!" he growled.

"Get him off me!" the rancher cried to his men as he winced in pain.

Three ranch hands pounced on Wolf, one of them throwing an arm around his throat. Wolf shook them off like a duck shedding water, despite his exhaustion from breaking Diablo. Two more attacked, but Wolf held his own, and one caught a sledgehammer punch and went down hard. Wolf picked the second one up and threw him into four more who were charging in.

Suddenly Wolf felt something hard slam into the

back of his head. Unfazed by the blow, he pivoted and sank his fingers into the shirt of a man holding a board. Swinging him in circular fashion, he let go, and the man went flying into the dirt.

"That's enough!" came a sharp voice.

Wolf turned to see a cowboy holding a double-barreled shotgun aimed at his chest. "Now you mount up and get out, Indian lover," the man said levelly.

Wolf glared at Walt Tomberlin with hate and then turned and mounted his horse. He rode away with a renewed fury boiling within him toward white men.

Chapter Two

Wolf Bixler's dislike of the whites had grown worse with the passing of time. White men were greedy, not trustworthy. But it was most difficult to adjust to the derogatory attitude of the whites toward Indians.

As the months away from the Comanches increased, he found himself continuously at odds with the whites. They made light of his Indian ways. The fights he was in were numerous, and he lost one job after another.

At one point, the miserable young man had returned to the Comanche stronghold to live, but the attempt was unsuccessful. Though he loved them, his white skin was an uncomfortable wedge between him and the red-skinned people.

Once again, he returned to the white man's world, though his hatred for them was growing more savage. He found himself in fights more frequently. In addition to being good with his fists, he was skilled with knife, spear, bow, rifle, and pistol. Sometimes men died as a result of the beatings he gave them. He would not kill in cold blood, but woe to the man who threatened him or tried to crowd him into a corner.

He had been put behind bars all over Texas and New Mexico, but with his intelligence, determination, and brawn, no jail had been able to hold him. Lawmen had hunted and haunted him, turning him into a feral, indomitable beast. They all agreed that the name Wolf fit him well.

*   *   *

The condemned man's thoughts came out of the past at the sight of Pedro walking away from the gallows, hammer in hand. His job was finished; the dismal structure was ready.

Sighing deeply, Wolf turned away from the barred window, dragging the heavy chain that joined his ankles. Sitting on the bunk, he ran his fingers through the thick mop of jet-black hair on his head.

He remembered what Wounded Hawk had once said after a burial ceremony for an old Comanche warrior. *Man is born to die, Little Wolf.* At forty years of age, Wolf's time had come.

How would he feel when that trapdoor gave way under his feet? What would it be like five seconds after the rope snapped his neck?

He felt his stomach growl. He would get nothing to eat before they hanged him. In the States, they at least would feed him first.

He rubbed his wrists where the shackles had chafed the skin, and let his mind wander back, recounting the series of events that had brought him to this moment.

Two months before, the white man's army and the Comanches were fighting on the Texas plains, the Indians slowly being overcome because of their lack of weapons and ammunition. Greedy whites were ever-present, ready to sell the red men guns and bullets, but the Comanches had no money.

Wolf had been working on a ranch near Waco, breaking mustangs, when a cowboy just in from that town rode up. Other men on the ranch had gathered around him. The cowboy had news of a Comanche village being wiped out by the army, some twenty miles due west of Waco. The cowboy's words cut Wolf's breath short: The village described was at Oak Creek, where the aged Wounded Hawk and Red Fawn lived.

He quickly mounted his horse and rode hard for the village, arriving in little more than an hour. There he found young Chief Iron Face and a few warriors moving slowly and somberly among the smoking ruins of the village. Bodies of old men and women, young squaws, and children were strewn about.

Wolf had dismounted slowly, his heart frozen in his chest. Iron Face lifted his eyes to the huge man as Wolf drew near. "Soldier coats did this, Wolf Bixler. Your white brothers."

"They are no brothers of mine," Wolf said with a cold, hard voice. "Have you seen—?"

"Wounded Hawk and his squaw are there," Iron Face cut in, pointing to a spot fifty feet away.

He hurried to where the crumpled, bloody bodies of the old couple lay. The aged chief had evidently tried to shield Red Fawn from the white man's bullets.

Wolf could feel his muscles constrict with rage, and his blood coursed faster through his veins. From behind him, Iron Face said, "They came while the squaws, children, and old men were alone. All the braves were out in hunting parties. We were first to return. When we arrived, we found one young boy barely alive. He said it was soldier coats from army post at Waco. The boy is now dead."

Wolf's gaze was on the lifeless forms of the two people who had been the only parents he had ever known.

Iron Face spoke again from behind him. "What kind of white-eyes beast makes war on the aged, and helpless women and children, Wolf Bixler?"

As Wolf slowly turned around, his teeth clenched. "I don't know, Iron Face. But I aim to find out."

The deep red sun was touching the western horizon when Wolf Bixler tamped the two mounds with the shovel and threw it aside. Standing over the graves, his six-foot-six-inch frame shook with fury. He would have vengeance.

An hour later, adopting a cool facade to mask his fury, he had ridden to the army post at Waco, where he learned that the leader of the raid had been Captain Leon Sightler. The captain, he was told by the sentry, was in town at one of the saloons, celebrating his victory. Wolf wheeled his horse and headed for Waco, half a mile away.

The town had five saloons. In the third one he entered, he found four uniformed men sitting at a table, laughing boisterously. One of them was trying to balance a half-empty whiskey bottle on his chin. The other patrons were joining in, laughing and talking loudly above the noise of a tinkling piano.

Wolf Bixler adjusted the gun belt on his waist and sidled up to the bar.

"What'll you have?" asked the bartender, a small, balding man.

"Do you know a Captain Leon Sightler?" Wolf asked in his deep, gravelly voice.

"Why, yes." The bartender nodded and then chuckled. "That's him over there with the whiskey bottle on his chin."

"Much obliged," said Wolf. "I'd like to buy a bottle of the stuff myself."

"A whole bottle? Whiskey?"

"Yeah. How much?"

"Six dollars, mister," said the bartender, lifting a bottle from a shelf behind the bar.

Wolf plunked down the money and picked up the bottle. Taking a few steps away from the bar, he stood where there was no obstruction between himself and the captain.

Leon Sightler had his head tilted·back and had just taken his hand away from the bottle that was balancing precariously on his chin. Wolf grasped his own bottle by the neck and hurled it at Sightler's. The onlookers were just breaking into applause when the bottles collided with a crash. Glass shattered in every direction, dumping whiskey in the captain's face, soaking his coat and shirt.

The piano stopped abruptly, as did the laughter and applause. Sightler was coughing and thumbing whiskey from his eyes. He blinked several times and then looked with surprise at the massive, bearded man standing there, black eyes filled with a virulent fury.

Eyeing Wolf with contempt, Sightler's companions, a lieutenant and two sergeants, scraped their chairs back and stood. But Wolf, fixing the captain with a glare like the stab of a bayonet, growled, "Are you the yellow-bellied coward who makes war on women and children?"

Sightler, drenched with whiskey, rose slowly from his chair. He looked a bit comical with his hair matted to his head. But before the captain could say anything, Lieutenant Jack Abbott pointed a stiff forefinger at Wolf and said, "You watch your mouth, big boy. There are four of us here."

"I wasn't talkin' to you, junior," Wolf rasped. "I was talkin' to the captain."

Abbott's features crimsoned. He started to speak when Sightler laid a hand on his shoulder. Eyeing Wolf with guarded speculation, the captain said, "I assume, mister, that you are referring to the Comanches at Oak Creek."

"You assume correctly," said the huge man in a threatening tone.

Leon Sightler himself was a good-sized man at six feet tall and just over two hundred pounds. He looked Wolf Bixler up and down with disdain. "What do you care about a bunch of dead savages?"

Wolf took a half step toward the dripping officer, his face revealing his gathering rage. "Two of those dead savages were my parents. They were eighty years old. What kind of threat were they to you and your yellow-bellied soldier boys?"

"Indians don't have to be a threat to come under my guns, big man," Sightler responded insolently. "All they have to be is Indians." Squinting as if to study Wolf's features, he said, "You're not a red man. How could they be your parents?"

"They adopted me," Wolf retorted levelly. "They were the only family I had, and you murdered them."

"*Murdered* them? How could I have murdered them? You can't murder an Indian, same as you can't murder a rattlesnake. Indians aren't human!"

Wolf Bixler's massive frame stiffened as the corners of his mouth pulled down hard. The onlookers began to scatter. Flicking his eyes both ways, Sightler looked at the men standing at his flank. Sergeants Dub Mills and

Edmund Curtin looked at Lieutenant Jack Abbott and then turned back to the huge bearded man.

Wolf Bixler took a step closer, eyes burning. Sightler shifted his stance, and his boot knocked against one of the broken bottles on the floor. The bottle was broken about midway down, with sharp, jagged edges, but the neck of the bottle was intact.

"Big tough soldiers, ain't you?" Wolf challenged. "You can slaughter helpless women. You can shoot tottering old men and defenseless children. But if you'd seen warriors comin', you would've had urgent business elsewhere. Snivelin' cowards. You wouldn't face a man."

Dub Mills blurted, "We'll face *you*!"

"One at a time, yellow-belly?"

Mills looked around at his friends for support.

Suddenly Leon Sightler snatched up the broken bottle and charged Wolf, aiming the jagged edges at his eyes. But Wolf sidestepped, dodging the weapon, and seized the captain's wrist. Just as Abbott came charging in, followed by both sergeants, Wolf twisted the bottle from his grip. Sightler stumbled, going off balance as the bottle shattered on the floor.

Wolf clubbed the lieutenant on the back of the neck, knocking him flat. Next in line was Curtin, who sent a fist solidly toward Wolf's jaw. Wolf flicked Curtin's fist away like he would a pesky fly and punched him savagely, piston-style. The man sailed across the room and slammed into a table, knocking it over.

At the same moment, Sightler brought a chair down violently on Wolf's back. But Wolf retaliated, pivoting and throwing a roundhouse punch to the captain's jaw, connecting with a violent cracking sound. The powerful blow sent Sightler reeling into a group of bystanders, and he fell, hitting his head on a table, and lay still.

Turning toward the remaining man, Wolf saw Dub Mills, wild-eyed, coming at him swinging a chair. He shot out his huge hand and grabbed the chair in midair, and Mills's face blanched, his mouth sagging in fear. Wolf jerked the chair from his hands and threw it aside.

Mills's head swiveled back and forth, searching for a place to hide. Wolf, looking at the sergeant coldly from

narrowed eyes, sank his fingers into Mills's shirt and
drew the other hand back, forming a fist. The blow
sounded like a flat rock dropping into mud. Mills went
flying across the room in a loose-jointed roll, finally
bumping against the bar and sagging to the floor.

The crowd gazed at Wolf, awed by his power and by
the ease with which he had disposed of his four attackers.

Looking at the four unconscious men, Wolf Bixler
growled to the onlookers, "You tell these sorry hunks of
slime to stay out of my way. Next time I see them, I
may lose my temper."

His anger vented, Wolf rode back to the ranch, mourn-
ing the loss of his parents.

At dawn the next day, he awoke in the bunkhouse to
find himself surrounded by eight uniformed men, each
holding a rifle on him. He sat up slowly, shaking his
head. Why was the army after him? He had been in
saloon brawls with soldiers before. Every man always
took his own knocks and forgot it.

Examining the soldiers' faces, Wolf saw a ninth man
shoulder his way between two of the others. He was
not in uniform but wore a tin star on his vest. "Mr.
Bixler," he said in an authoritative voice, "I am Waco's
marshal, Stuart Jarrell. You are under arrest."

Wolf squared his shoulders and stared at the young
lawman with black, penetrating eyes. "What for?"

The marshal, a tall, lean man, pulled a slip of paper
from his shirt pocket and unfolded it. "I have here a
warrant for your arrest. You did strike a Captain Leon
Sightler last night at the Texas Rose Saloon, did you
not?"

Wolf rubbed sleep from his eyes and replied, "Yeah.
He and three other yellow-bellied murderers. You're
arrestin' me for that fight?"

"Not for the fight itself, Mr. Bixler," came Jarrell's
level answer, "but for the results of the fight."

Wolf swore and shook his head. "Okay, okay," he
mumbled with disgust, "how much are the damages?
Tell the saloon owner I'll pay whatever it is."

"It's not that simple," said the steely-eyed marshal.
"You left the four soldiers unconscious in the saloon.

Captain Sightler never regained consciousness. He died in the post infirmary at three o'clock this morning."

Wolf rubbed a palm across his face. "You're arrestin' me for killin' him?"

"Yes, sir."

"For murder?"

"The charge is manslaughter, Mr. Bixler."

"Now look," Wolf argued, "I didn't go in there to kill him. I just went in there to talk with him."

"All of that will come out in the trial, sir," said the young lawman. "My job is not to hear your case. My job is to arrest you and incarcerate you so that you can stand trial."

There was an unnatural tightness in Wolf Bixler's throat. "I don't know that I want to stand trial."

"I'm here to see that you don't get a choice in the matter, Mr. Bixler," Jarrell said, his voice sounding like a ripsaw cutting through a nail. "And these men with their guns pointed at you are here to back me up. Now you can come along peaceably and stand trial, or take eight slugs and be buried. That is the only choice you have."

After staring at the marshal for a few moments with smoldering eyes, Wolf slowly pushed back the covers, set his bare feet on the floor, and stood up.

While Wolf dressed with eight muzzles pointed at him, Jarrell warned, "I am aware of your reputation for breaking jail and manhandling lawmen, Mr. Bixler. Don't try it with me, because I'll kill you."

It had taken the jury exactly five minutes to deliberate Wolf Bixler's fate and return to the courtroom with the verdict. He was pronounced guilty of manslaughter.

Judge Roxborough P. Fairchild called the defendant before the bench and looked him square in the eye. "Wolf Bixler," he said sternly, "you have been convicted of manslaughter. Your uncouth and brutal tactics have cost the United States Army a fine and courageous officer. This court hereby sentences you to twenty years imprisonment. You will be confined at the military prison on the post here in Waco until the time that a federal penitentiary is constructed in this vicinity."

Wiping a hand over his brow, Fairchild added, "It is the concern/of this court that you learn a lesson from this, Mr. Bixler. It is not lawful in a civilized society for a man to attack another human being, much less to take his life."

Wolf regarded the judge impassively. "That depends on what color your skin is, doesn't it, Your Honor?" he asked.

Fairchild's facial features drew tight, his lips turning purple. "You, sir, are on the verge of being in contempt of this court. You will please explain that remark!"

"It wasn't a remark, Your Honor," Wolf chided. "It was a question. If your high and mighty statement is true about law in a civilized society, why don't you arrest every one of those murderers who rode into the Comanche village at Oak Creek and slaughtered unarmed and helpless women, children, and old men?"

"This case is finished!" snapped the furious judge, banging the gavel down hard. "And this court is adjourned! Take the prisoner away!"

As a precaution, Marshal Stuart Jarrell had placed Wolf Bixler in leg irons, in addition to a double set of handcuffs. While leading his prisoner from the courtroom, Jarrell was approached by one of Waco's leading businessmen. "Is what I'm hearing so, Stu?" he asked. "We're going to lose you?"

"Yes, sir," answered Jarrell. "I've just been appointed as a United States marshal."

Chapter Three

Wolf Bixler listened to another round of coarse laughter filtering through his window from the prison yard near Mexico City. Rising from the bunk, he made his way to the narrow opening and peered through the bars. The sun's rim had appeared in blazing glory on the eastern horizon, casting streamers of light skyward. He figured he had only thirty minutes before the guards would come for him.

When he saw the object of the laughter below, Wolf grew furious. The guards were gathered around the gallows, looking up at one of their cohorts who had mounted the scaffold. He was gripping the hangman's knot, holding it as if the noose were around his neck. In mockery of the man who was about to hang, he pretended he was gagging, his tongue extended and his eyes bulging.

Bixler swore and returned to his bunk. If he had to die, he wished it could have been in Texas instead of Mexico.

He thought back to his days in the military prison in Waco. In his mind's eye he could see the twinkling eyes of his cell mate, Gilbert Salazar, as the fat Mexican pressed his swarthy face close and said eagerly, "Señor Wolf, I have been hearing things!"

"Like what?" Wolf had asked, turning his face from the man's foul breath.

"I have learned from the other prisoners that you are an expert at breaking out of jails and prisons."

"I've crashed out of a few," Wolf admitted tonelessly. "Fact is, I'm already thinkin' on a plan to get out of here."

"Good!" exclaimed Salazar in a hoarse whisper. "You will take me with you."

Wolf shook his head. "Nope."

"No?" The fat man's face pinched tight. "But you must, Señor Wolf! As long as you are going, why cannot I go with you?"

"I work alone, Gilbert," Wolf said flatly. "You would be a hindrance."

"Oh, no, Señor Wolf!" the Mexican said, gripping Wolf's big, trunklike arm. "I would not get in the way. I would be lots of help!"

Wolf regarded him with scorn, pulling his arm from the man's fingers. "I said I'm going alone," he growled.

Gilbert Salazar knew better than to push the short-tempered giant any further. Rather, he thought quietly on the situation for the rest of the day. After the lights were out that night and they lay in the darkness, he said quietly, "Señor Wolf?"

Wolf Bixler grunted. "Huh?"

"I need to explain something to you."

"Wait till morning."

"I cannot. This is extremely important."

"I'm sleepy, Gilbert," Wolf said in an impatient tone. "It can wait till tomorrow."

"I just thought you might be interested in why I want you to take me with you when you break out."

"That's not hard to figure," mumbled the big man.

"No, you do not understand," Gilbert said, sitting up in his bunk. Looking at Wolf's vague outline across the cramped cell, he continued, "I want to enjoy spending my wealth."

"Mmm? Wealth?"

"Sí, Señor Wolf. Fifty thousand dollars worth of gold. If you will take me with you, I will give you half."

Wolf Bixler sat up. "You have fifty thousand dollars in gold?"

"Sí."

"You're lyin' to me, Gilbert."

"No, Señor Wolf. It is the truth. I will share it with you. One half."

"Where is it?"

"It is buried in the floor of an old barn in Puebla, a town eighty miles southeast of Mexico City."

"How did you get it?"

"My brothers and I stole it from the government shipment. We buried it in the barn, planning to dig it up and divide it among ourselves after the Federales gave up looking for it and the thieves. A few weeks later, we robbed a mule train carrying a secret shipment of gold. We did not know the Federales were following close. There was a gun battle. I saw all four of my brothers killed."

"How'd you get away?" Wolf queried.

"During the shooting I ran under cover of the dust and smoke of the guns. I headed north, and about fifty miles out of Mexico City I found some travelers going to Texas. I went with them to escape the Federales."

"So how'd you get here?"

"I broke into a store here in Waco one night two years ago. I needed food and clothes. The owner caught me while I was in the store. I have three years to go on my sentence. Please, Señor Wolf. Take me with you. We will go to Mexico together, and I will give you half of the gold."

Wolf Bixler's mind was churning. He thought of Chief Iron Face and the Comanche tribe's war with the white man's army. He knew what the gold would mean to the Comanches. Twenty-five thousand dollars would buy many weapons and a lot of ammunition.

Wolf realized Gilbert Salazar could be lying. It might just be a scheme to get himself out of prison on Wolf's shirttail. On the other hand, it could be true. There was no way to know. Certainly twenty-five thousand dollars was worth the gamble. Besides, he had to go *somewhere* when he broke out of prison. It might as well be Mexico.

Speaking through the gloom of the cell, Wolf said, "Gilbert, you wouldn't make all this up just to get out of here, would you?"

"Oh no, Señor Wolf!" the fat man responded. "You are big and strong. You would crush this *mejicano* like a cockroach if I was lying."

"That's right," breathed Wolf. "Like a cockroach."

"I am telling the truth, señor. Believe me. If you take me with you, Wolf Bixler will soon be a rich gringo."

Within a week, Wolf was ready to go.

He had observed during his time in the prison that every night between nine and ten o'clock, a water wagon came into the army post. Its tank was about eight feet long and about twelve feet in circumference. Two inmates from the prison were always chosen to unload the water.

The round, lidded opening on top of the wagon's tank was large enough for a man even of Wolf's size to slip through.

The post had a water tank that stood on stilts at a level slightly higher than the tank on the wagon. Standing on a narrow platform on the side of the wagon, one man would dip water in a bucket. He would hand it to the other man, who stood on a similar platform and poured the water into the post's tank. Using two buckets, it would take them about an hour to transfer the water from one tank to the other.

The two men who unloaded the water were chosen in a very simple way. In the prison's mess hall, the long eating tables were lined with crude wooden chairs, exactly enough to accommodate the inmates. Two chairs situated at the end of one table were marked with the words "water boys." Hence, the last two men to enter the mess hall and find seats were elected.

Wolf's plan was for him and Gilbert to be the stragglers. The post was dimly lit at night, which would serve to conceal their actions. But they would have to time things right to overpower the single driver on the side of the water wagon opposite the guard tower. They would knock him out after they unloaded the water, remove his shirt and hat, and then push him inside the empty tank. Wearing the driver's garments, Salazar would drive the wagon out of the post while Wolf rode inside the tank with the unconscious driver. The two of them would then steal a couple of saddled horses from the hitch rail in front of one of the saloons in town and ride for Mexico.

When Bixler explained the scheme to his dark-skinned cell mate, the Mexican grinned broadly. "Señor Wolf, you are one smart hombre! Your plan will work. I am sure of it."

Gilbert Salazar's prophecy was accurate. Wolf's contrivance went off without a hitch.

The two men had ridden hard for Mexico, stopping only long enough to steal guns, food, and a hunting knife on the way. Crossing the Rio Grande at night nine days later, they had moved southward toward Puebla. After nearly three weeks of pushing their mounts to the limit, they arrived at the edge of town late in the afternoon on November 13.

Salazar had led Wolf into a dense thicket of trees and said, "It is best that you wait here, Señor Wolf. My people are of a very suspicious nature. It is best that they do not see you."

Wolf looked at him with misgiving. "Where are you going?"

"To the barn, of course."

"You mean you're going to dig up the gold by yourself?"

"Oh, no, Señor Wolf," said the fat Mexican. "I just want to look inside and make sure nothing is disturbed. Anyone who might see me would think nothing of it. I am only one of hundreds of *mejicanos*. But you! Ha! You are gringo. Large gringo! They would spot you immediately. You would arouse their suspicions."

Wolf was feeling uneasy about the situation. He had no basis for his feeling—it was just there. Shrugging it off, he told himself he had no reason to believe that Salazar was pulling anything on him. "Okay," he said. "You scout it out."

Salazar nodded. "I will return soon."

Leaving his horse with Wolf, the fat man walked toward the sleepy town of Puebla. Wolf watched him till he disappeared on a dusty street between stucco buildings.

The sun dipped low behind the jagged outline of the vast mountain peaks to the west. Wolf watched the dark-skinned people milling about the edge of town, but saw no sign of Gilbert Salazar.

Soon it was dusk, and the last dying light of the sun was struggling against darkness. Still there was no Gilbert Salazar. Wolf was nearly convinced Salazar had pulled a fast one on him, when he saw a vague form detach itself from the buildings and move in his direction.

Drawing near the thicket, the Mexican said, "Psst! Señor Wolf, are you still in there?"

Wolf swore at Salazar, asking where he had been and why he had been gone so long.

"I am sorry, Señor Wolf," he said apologetically. "There were some Federales moving about town. I did not want them to see me. I had to wait in the barn until dark. I have good news, though! The spot where the gold is buried has not been disturbed. You are only moments away from being a rich man! Let us go."

The Mexican suggested that it would be best if they went on foot, since on horseback they would be more conspicuous. By walking, they could stay in the shadows all the way to the barn and never be seen.

Within fifteen minutes, the two men had darted past the last stucco house and approached the old barn. It was a frame structure and looked to Wolf as though a good wind could level it.

As they moved in the darkness to the door, he said, "How are we going to see what we're doin'?"

"I have taken care of that matter," Gilbert replied. "I stole two lanterns off a porch while coming here. Matches, too."

When the Mexican pulled the latch and swung the door outward, the rusty hinges protested loudly. The two men stepped into the darkness, and Salazar closed and latched the door behind them.

Fumbling in the blackness, Salazar said, "One moment, Señor Wolf, and I will light a lantern."

Wolf heard the scratch of a match and then saw the

Mexican in the flare of the light. In an instant the place was flooded with a dim yellow glow as the wick came alive. Eerie, dancing shadows were all about.

Salazar set the lantern on a barrel and then went to a vertical wooden beam that supported the rickety, sagging roof. From a nail on the beam, he took a second lantern, lighted it, and then hung it back on the nail. Wolf noticed that the entire floor was covered with old straw. "Now, Señor Wolf," Salazar said, crooking his finger, "if you will step over here."

Wolf had taken two steps when he heard the rustle of feet on the straw behind him. He was starting to turn when three imposing figures emerged from the shadows in front of him, each aiming a black muzzle on his upper torso. The man behind him took Wolf's sidearm and the long-bladed knife he wore in a scabbard on his left side.

Wolf glared at Salazar with fierce, blazing eyes.

The fat Mexican laughed fiendishly. "These are my four brothers, Señor Wolf. Pretty good, eh? They came back from the dead! But of course, I am forgetting my manners. I must introduce my brothers to you."

The antagonism in Wolf's eyes was almost tangible. But he was nearly as angry at himself for not heeding his instincts earlier.

Motioning to the man behind Wolf, Salazar said, "Come around here, Salvadore. Señor Wolf will not go for the door. He knows he cannot outrun bullets."

Salvadore Salazar had jammed Wolf's revolver under his belt. Carrying the knife in one hand and his own gun in the other, he sauntered around the big man in a cocky manner. Looking him up and down, he grinned, and then joined the other three brothers, who stood abreast ten feet from Wolf.

Gilbert Salazar stood just out of arm's reach to the left of his captive. At the same distance to Wolf's right was the upright beam that held one of the lanterns.

Pointing out each brother with his stubby finger, Gilbert Salazar said, "As you heard, Señor Wolf, this is my brother Salvadore. The others are Rubin, Hermando, and Julio." Bringing his dark eyes back to Wolf's face, he added, "And you, Señor Wolf, are a fool."

Wolf Bixler's lips were drawn thin and curved downward by anger. "So you used me to get you out of prison," he said frigidly, "but why did you bring me clear across Mexico?"

Chuckling, Gilbert Salazar said, "Eluding the gringo authorities is very difficult, Señor Wolf. Traveling across Mexico is also very dangerous. With a big, rough man like Wolf Bixler for a companion, Gilbert Salazar was much more certain of escaping the gringo lawmen and much safer in traveling across this country." Exposing his teeth in a broad grin, he added, "And, of course, there never was any gold."

Ignoring the last statement, which was no surprise at this point, Wolf asked, "Are you tellin' me that as a citizen of this country, you are afraid to travel across it?"

Hunching his shoulders, Gilbert replied, "It is dangerous to travel alone, señor. However, the greatest threat was from the gringos from Texas."

"What are you talkin' about? You're in Mexico."

"You have not heard of El Presidente Sebastian Lerdo de Tejada's agreement with your President Grant?"

When Wolf said nothing, Salazar continued.

"El Presidente Tejada has entered into a foolish extradition agreement. Our Federales can cross the border to pursue and arrest *mejicano* criminals, and gringo lawmen can do the same thing when gringo criminals flee into Mexico. Both are allowed to take the criminals back to their own countries to be prosecuted without hindrance from local authorities, no questions asked."

Taking a deep breath, Salazar said, "My brothers and I are in total opposition to that swine Tejada. I have learned today that my brothers are part of Porfirio Díaz's revolutionary army. The revolutionaries are about to overthrow the Tejada regime. With Díaz as leader of Mexico, there will be no more extradition deals with the stinking gringos."

The brothers voiced their agreement in unison.

"At this moment," Gilbert Salazar went on, "our

country is stuck with the extradition covenant. Tejada! *Bah!*" He spat on the floor and then said, "Señor Wolf, you killed an officer of the United States Army. I knew the authorities might come into Mexico after you. Since I am not wanted by the law here, but I *am* wanted in Texas, they might come after me, too. With your experience and capability at eluding lawmen, I wanted you with me all the way."

Wolf Bixler swore under his breath. He had played the fool indeed.

"Of course, now you must die," Salazar said coldly. "Since no one in Puebla has seen you, we can kill you and bury you in the floor of this barn."

"It will take a plenty big hole," Rubin Salazar interjected, smiling in a tight, evil way.

Ignoring Rubin's interruption, Gilbert Salazar said, "Since you will be dead and buried, Señor Wolf, there will be no trace of you. If the gringo lawmen come to Puebla looking for us, they can ask everyone in town. No one has seen a bearded, mountain-sized gringo in Puebla. No one has noticed me, either. The search of the gringo lawmen will end here. My brothers will hide me out in the mountains until the gringos have come and gone. Then I will be a free man."

While the fat Mexican was talking, Wolf Bixler was carefully examining the area around him. He had to find a way to get out of this predicament. Then he saw a heavy chain, six feet in length, hanging from a nail on the beam holding one of the lanterns.

While talking, Gilbert Salazar had moved closer to his intended victim, apparently feeling safe with all four brothers holding their guns on the captive man. Wolf realized that Salazar was now well within reach of his left hand. And the chain could be reached with one step.

Gauging the distance between him and the four brothers, Wolf seized Gilbert Salazar, turning him face-forward toward his brothers while holding him by the back of his collar. It took the foursome a few seconds to react, and by the time they realized what was happening, Wolf had the chain in hand, holding it by one end.

Shoving Gilbert Salazar's corpulent body forward, Wolf violently swung the chain. Its tip struck Julio's gunhand, gouging into the flesh. Julio howled, dropping the gun, and stood in a state of shock, holding the injured hand with the other, eyes fixed on the raw meat of the wound.

The other three momentarily froze for fear of hitting their brother Gilbert if they fired.

The chain hissed savagely through the air again as Wolf pushed Gilbert Salazar farther toward his brothers. It slashed across Hermando's face, taking off his nose. Blood spurted as Hermando collapsed. Rubin and Salvadore jumped back and fired their guns at the same time, trying to hit Wolf, but both slugs ripped into Gilbert instead.

Wolf pushed the limp body of Gilbert Salazar into Rubin, who was thumbing back his hammer to fire again, and the impact knocked Rubin down. Wolf hurled the chain at Salvadore, who was also preparing to fire. The chain locked on his neck midway in its length, winding one end around his head. The last link split his upper lip. He fell backward, his gun firing harmlessly.

At the same moment, Wolf saw Julio leaning over to retrieve his gun with his good hand. The big man dived for the gun, beating Julio to it.

The hole in Hermando's face where his nose had been was pumping blood. But he brought his gun to bear from where he lay on the floor. Just as Hermando fired, Wolf rolled and shot him through the heart. Hermando's bullet chewed into dirt.

Both Rubin and Salvadore were now bringing their guns up while rising to their knees. The gun in Wolf's hand belched fire twice, and both men fell.

Wolf turned to see Julio coming up with Hermando's gun. Taking quick aim, he shot him in the chest, and Julio staggered sideways toward the barrel, knocking the lantern over. It crashed to the floor, instantly igniting the straw.

Julio still gripped Hermando's gun. Balancing on rubbery legs, he lifted it, pointing the muzzle toward his assailant.

Wolf shot him again. This time Julio went down dead.

Fire was spreading fast, and the barn was filling with smoke. Wolf headed for the door, but just before he reached it, it was flung open. He was staring into the guns of a half-dozen Federales.

Chapter Four

The sunlight coming through the narrow window was now casting a slanted rectangular shape on the back wall of Wolf Bixler's cell. The shadows of the bars lay in uneven lines.

Two large rats chased each other across the cell and then disappeared into a hole in the floor.

Wolf thought of how he had been convicted of murder in the Mexican courtroom the day after his arrest. In spite of his pleas of self-defense, he was pronounced guilty of murdering all five Salazar brothers. The judge had sentenced him to hang one week later, November 21, 1876.

Suddenly he heard heavy footsteps in the corridor, accompanied by lighter ones. A cold chill slithered down the big man's spine as the footsteps stopped outside his cell door. In the moment before the lock rattled, Wolf was aware of the wind whipping through the outside window, whining around the bars with a haunting, abrasive moan.

The door squealed on its hinges as it swung open. César Ramos, the prison warden, was framed in the doorway, flanked by four armed guards and a short, timid-looking priest.

Wolf Bixler unfolded himself off the bunk and stood to his full height, looking at Ramos, a man in his early sixties. The hair on his head was gray, flecked with black, and his complexion was ashen.

Wolf squared his huge shoulders, rattling the chains that joined his wrists. Ramos gazed intensely at the big man as he said levelly, "It is time, Bixler."

The hair stirred on the back of Wolf's neck. His eyes held Ramos's with a black hatred, the power of it finally driving the warden's eyes away.

Stepping aside, Ramos motioned for the priest. The small Mexican moved into the cell, bearing a prayer book and a dangling rosary. With a voice that fit his frail frame, he said, "I will hear your confession, my son."

The black hatred in Wolf Bixler's eyes was now concentrated on the priest. "I ain't confessin' nothin' to you. I'm not interested in your religion. I'll face this on my own."

"I really think you should talk to the padre," Ramos said confidently.

"*You* talk to him, Ramos," snapped the towering prisoner. "You're the murderer here, not me. I'm no doubt goin' to hell myself. But when I get there, I'll tell them you're comin', too."

The priest cleared his throat, awed by the size and gruff manner of the prisoner. Producing a pencil from his long, black robe, he ran a finger under his clerical collar and said timorously, "I . . . I am in charge of the cemetery here. I need your name. I mean . . . I mean your real name. There will be a small grave marker. It . . . uh . . . it should have your real name on it."

"My name is Wolf Bixler."

Batting his eyelids, the priest said, "I assume Wolf to be a nickname. What is your *real* first name?"

Attempting to help, César Ramos spoke up. "What the padre is saying, Bixler, is that you must have a given name. He assumes, as I do, that someone started calling you Wolf because . . . well, because of your mannerisms."

"I was raised by Comanche Indians," Wolf said gruffly. "They gave me my name. It is Wolf Bixler."

Jotting it nervously on a slip of paper in his prayer book, the priest said without looking up, "I will need your birth date, Señor Bixler."

"I have no idea what that is," responded the hulking

man. "I only know that I have lived thirty-five years
since the Comanches found me and took me in. They
told me I was about five years old at the time."

Nervously, the black-robed man nodded, jotted something, and stepped aside.

"All right, Bixler," said Ramos. "The hangman is
waiting. Let us be going. We must first shackle your
hands behind your back."

The warden turned and nodded to the guards. Two of
them stepped into the cell, while the other two remained in the corridor, guns ready.

Raising his huge hands, Wolf shook the chain at the
two who approached him. They halted in their tracks,
faces registering fear.

"What are you afraid of, gentlemen?" Wolf chided. "I
am one man. You come for me with an army."

One of the guards regained his composure and
whipped out his revolver. Pointing it between Wolf's
eyes, he said through his teeth, "You will stand still and
allow my compadre to unlock the wristband of your left
hand. You will then place both hands behind your back
while he locks it on your wrist again. If you make even
one small move, I will paint the wall of this cell with
your blood and leave fragments of your brain for the
rats to feast upon."

The air was tense as the guard named Pablo Acosta
held the muzzle of his gun steady between Wolf Bixler's dark eyes. Wolf noted that in Acosta's haste to put
the gun on him, he had neglected to cock the hammer.
Moving with the speed of a cougar, Wolf pulled the
chain taut between his wrists and brought it up violently, catching Acosta's hand where it gripped the
revolver. The weapon flew out of his hand.

Before anyone could move, the huge man stepped
behind the guard, dropped his shackled hands over
Pablo Acosta's head, and drew the short length of chain
up tight under the man's chin. Acosta gagged, ejecting
a choking sound, his frightened eyes bulging. He clawed
at the chain with curled fingers.

The other guard in the cell went for the gun in his
holster.

"No!" Wolf roared. "Touch that gun and I'll break his neck!"

The guards outside had begun to raise their guns, but checked the impulse. The priest's face took on the color of dead ashes. He crossed himself and began mumbling a prayer. César Ramos ran a shaky palm over his face.

Holding the chain tight against Acosta's throat, Wolf barked, "You, guards! Put down your guns!"

The two in the corridor looked cautiously at each other.

"Don't even think it!" blustered the huge man. "Even if you shoot me, I'll have time to snap this man's spine! And don't forget, I've got nothin' to lose. Your hangman is waitin' for me."

Wolf's mind was working fast. He watched the two guards lay their guns on the corridor floor and then commanded them to step back against the opposite wall. Looking at the other guard in the cell, he said, "Now you pick up your revolver and stick it in my belt."

Pablo Acosta was still gagging and choking. His face was turning purple.

The guard stepped to where his gun lay on the floor. As he bent to pick it up, the warden blurted, "No! Do not give him the gun!"

The man froze.

Turning to the desperate prisoner, Ramos said, "Your reputation has followed you to Mexico City, Bixler. On the day of your trial, a gringo here told us about you. We know that no jail or prison in your country has been able to hold you. That is why you were put in chains to begin with. Now I must keep you from escaping this prison."

Wolf Bixler's angry, determined eyes bored into Ramos's face. "You will do as I tell you," he hissed. "Or this man dies!"

A deep moan came from Acosta's mouth.

"I'm going to have that gun, Warden," Wolf said. "You're leavin' this prison as my hostage. I will not harm you if you cooperate. Now tell the man to pick up the gun and put it under my belt."

César Ramos moved his head back and forth slowly.

Acosta tried to speak, but could make no sound.

"I will not do it," Ramos said doggedly. "You are not getting the gun. Neither are you leaving this prison."

Wolf pulled the chain tighter against Acosta's throat. The helpless guard's eyes closed and then bulged as he choked in agony. He looked at the warden pleadingly.

Ramos seemed suddenly without feeling. Blandly, he said to Wolf, "You may as well release him. You are going nowhere."

Wolf Bixler's granite features darkened. He jerked the chain hard, and Acosta's mouth pulled tight in a grimace.

"I ain't kiddin', Ramos!" growled Wolf. "I'll kill him!"

The warden's face was impassive. "You can kill him, Bixler," he said, barely opening his mouth, "but you will remain in this prison, and you will still hang."

Disbelief registered in Pablo Acosta's eyes, and a piteous whine came from his throat. Wolf released pressure on the chain so the man could speak.

Gagging and choking out the words, Acosta pleaded, "Please, warden! He means it! Do not let him kill me! I do not want to die!"

César Ramos spoke to the guards in the corridor. "Pick up your guns. Señor Bixler will not escape."

The guards crossed the narrow corridor and retrieved their weapons, and the guard in the cell picked up his revolver.

A wave of despair washed over Wolf Bixler. The warden had a heart of cold stone. Pablo Acosta's life meant nothing to him. Ramos most certainly would allow the guard to die before he would let his prisoner escape.

Wolf's massive frame relaxed, and reluctantly he released the terrified guard, who threw his hands to his throat, coughing and choking. Acosta shot Ramos a malevolent glare and then left the cell and hurried down the corridor.

The warden snatched the revolver from the other guard's hand, snapped back the hammer, and aimed it at Wolf Bixler's nose, holding the gun with both hands.

From the side of his mouth he said to the guard, "Unlock the band on his left wrist."

Wolf regarded Ramos with cold eyes as the guard obeyed and released the left wrist. For a brief instant, Wolf thought of trying again while his hands were not bound together, but he quickly dismissed the notion. He was sure Ramos would squeeze the trigger at the slightest irregular movement. At least by walking to the gallows he could stay in this world a few moments longer. He submitted, allowing the guard to lock his wrists behind his back. Sure enough, old man Death was going to get him today.

Shuffling with the weight and metallic rattle of the heavy leg irons, Wolf Bixler followed César Ramos down the corridor and out the door. The priest, walking behind the prisoner and the three guards, brought up the rear.

The solemn procession descended the stone staircase to the ground and then turned and rounded the corner of the building. The cold wind gusted into their faces. When the gallows came into sight, Wolf's knees buckled slightly, but he forced himself on.

The priest began to pray audibly in Spanish.

Six guards were standing at attention near the wooden staircase of the gallows. On the platform above, José Villa was positioned next to the trapdoor, a smug look on his swarthy face. The noose swayed menacingly in the wind.

The rattle of the condemned man's leg chain echoed off the stone of the prison walls. The monotone of the priest's voice irritated Wolf. He abruptly turned to the short man and rasped, "Don't pray for me! Pray for the warden and that hangman. They'll have to face me in hell."

The boom of the huge man's voice startled the priest, and he swallowed hard and was silent.

As the procession reached the grotesque wooden structure, Ramos halted, the others following suit. Turning to the condemned man, Ramos said, "Will you climb the steps on your own, Bixler, or will the guards have to prod you with their weapons?"

Eyeing the warden with contempt, Wolf said, "I can make it on my own. Think of it when you pillow your head tonight, Ramos. You won't live forever. I'll be waitin' for you down yonder. Maybe my hands won't be shackled then."

The warden did not comment, but quietly pointed to the thirteen stairs.

Wolf's knees felt rubbery as he began to climb. The chain on his ankles forced him to move one step at a time, bringing each foot to each creaky step. The going was slow, allowing his hatred for the Mexicans to grow within him.

As he reached the third step, Wolf saw two hawks in flight overhead. They wheeled against the unfeeling sky and then rode the wind currents out of sight. Wolf yearned for that freedom, appreciating it as he never had before.

His mind flashed back to his childhood when he used to run across the grassy plains of west Texas with the Indian children. He had not a care in the world in those days. He had been happy. And free. And alive.

But now, under the cold Mexican sun, each step he climbed carried him closer to the clammy hands of Death.

Nearing the top, the condemned man set his eyes on the dark figure that stood on the platform. The vile hangman held a black hood in his hand, its color matching his clothing, even to the flat-crowned hat on his head. Wolf could tell from the look in José Villa's eyes that the man enjoyed his job.

The deadly noose swayed in the cold wind as Wolf approached the trapdoor.

With a vindictive sneer on his dark face, Villa motioned for Wolf to step onto the trapdoor, and as he did, Wolf felt it give slightly under his weight. Villa touched his shoulders, centering him over it and then facing him forward.

Wolf could see the enthralled faces of the prisoners observing the execution from their barred windows. He dropped his line of sight to the warden and the guards who stood below. He could hear the little priest praying aloud again, but could not see him.

When the hangman moved close, bearing the black hood, Wolf shook his head. "No hood," he said flatly.

"You must wear a hood," Villa insisted. "It is regulation."

As Villa raised the hood to place it on the prisoner's head, Wolf blared, "*I said no hood!*"

"José!" called the warden from the ground. "Leave the hood off."

Leaning close to his victim, Villa said in a low tone, "Why do you refuse the hood, señor? It is only meant as a gesture of mercy."

"I want to see hell before I get there, that's why," retorted the doomed man.

The hangman chuckled wickedly. "Well, let's not keep you waiting."

Villa took hold of the swaying noose and quickly lowered it over the big man's head. It settled across his chest and shoulders. Then Villa yanked it up tight around his throat, scratching the skin of Wolf's neck.

As the Mexican stepped back, Wolf's black eyes flashed fire, looking at him across an abyss of savage hatred. The hangman shrugged his shoulders, gave Wolf an insolent grin, and pivoted.

With his feet planted firmly on the trapdoor and the scratchy rope pulling at his neck, Wolf Bixler watched José Villa ceremoniously descend the stairs and take his position at the lever. Placing his hand on it, the hangman looked to the warden for the signal.

Bixler felt a wave of nausea run through him, and his heart quickened pace. He swallowed hard, causing the prickly fibers of the rope to stab his Adam's apple. Though the November wind was cold, his brow was beaded with sweat.

Wolf remembered from watching Villa earlier this morning that there was a delay of about two seconds between the throwing of the lever and the release of the trapdoor. His eyes were on Ramos, waiting for the signal.

The warden swung a glance up at Wolf, tall against

the sky, his dark features rigid. The wind flapped his pants legs and toyed with his tousled black hair.

Slowly and methodically, Ramos turned his face toward José Villa and nodded.

Wolf Bixler's mouth went dry. His entire body went numb.

Then he heard the lever snap.

Chapter Five

The stagecoach from Austin, where Stuart Jarrell had been made federal marshal, rolled to a halt in front of the Lone Star Stage Company office in Waco on November 20, 1876. United States marshal Stuart Jarrell alighted and took his single bag from the driver, who was up on the rack. Looking up and down the street, the marshal shook his head in puzzlement and started across the street.

"Howdy, Stu!" called an elderly man, crossing from the opposite direction. "How's the U.S. marshal business?"

"Well, I'm just getting a start in it, Mr. Wiggins," Jarrell replied with a warm smile, "but I think I'm going to like it."

"We miss you around here, son," said Wiggins, "but Marshal Foss is doing a fine job, fine job. He just ain't Stu Jarrell, no he isn't. There's only one of them."

Laughing, Jarrell said, "I guess the world could only stand one Stuart Jarrell at a time!"

"Where you gonna make your home now, son?" queried the old gentleman.

"Right here in Waco," Jarrell told him. "I'll receive my assignments out of the Austin office, but I'll still hang my hat right here."

"Well, that's plumb good news, yes it is," cackled Wiggins. "Guess I'll get to see you from time to time."

"Sure will," Jarrell answered.

With a twinkle in his eye, the silver-haired gent said, "You and Miss Peggy gonna get hitched up pretty soon?"

"Why, uh . . . yes," Jarrell said with a hint of bewilderment. "Real soon, now."

"She's a mighty fine young woman, that Miss Peggy," Wiggins remarked with conviction. "You're a dadburned lucky man, yes you are." Elbowing the marshal with a bony arm, he winked and added, "Good thing for you I ain't sixty years younger. I'd give you some competition."

"I sure lucked out there, didn't I?" laughed Jarrell, moving on. "See you later!"

The old man nodded and hobbled on his way.

Jarrell entered the town marshal's office to say hello to Bruce Foss, who had taken Jarrell's former job, but the man was not there. Moving down the street, Jarrell greeted people along the way and answered questions much like those asked by old man Wiggins.

Leaving the main street, the young lawman walked two blocks and entered the small house where he lived. Dropping the bag on the bed, he left the house and walked back to Main Street, rented a horse from the hostler, and rode toward the army post.

While riding the half mile to the post, Stuart Jarrell wondered if his worst fears had come true. Peggy knew he was coming in on today's Austin stage, and the stage had been right on time. Yet she had not been there to meet him.

When he rode through the gate at the army post, Jarrell temporarily laid aside his thoughts of Peggy Garner. He would be seeing her tonight, and his question would be answered then.

Colonel George Barber, commandant of the Waco post, welcomed Jarrell warmly. Closing his office door, he said, "Sit down, Stu. I assume you're all sworn in and a full-fledged government man now."

"Yes, sir," answered the tall, rawboned man, sitting in a wooden chair in front of the colonel's desk.

Barber sat down behind the desk and opened a humidor. Extending it to Jarrell, he said, "Cigar?"

"No, thanks," Jarrell answered.

The colonel bit the end off one for himself, replaced

the lid of the humidor, and said, "Well! What brings you out here?"

"I received my first assignment, sir," Jarrell replied in a serious tone. "Just thought you might like to know about it. I'm only in Waco for one day, so I thought I'd drop by."

There was genuine interest in the colonel's eyes.

"I know Wolf Bixler's escape was an embarrassment to you, sir," proceeded Jarrell. "I thought you would like to know that I'm going after him."

Barber's eyebrows arched. "Wolf Bixler?"

"Yes, sir."

"You did say *I*, not we?"

"Yes, sir."

"Is that wise? I mean . . . well, you have certainly proven yourself capable of tracking and apprehending outlaws as Waco's marshal. But Wolf Bixler is a self-contained army all by himself. Shouldn't you be taking a battalion with you?"

Jarrell smiled. "The Austin office let me make my own decision about that, sir. They would not have given me a battalion, of course. Bixler is a federal fugitive, so he must be pursued by federal lawmen. They did offer to supply me with two other men, though."

"That would be better than going alone, wouldn't it?"

"Not in my way of thinking, sir. You see, Bixler has gone into Mexico."

"Oh," said Barber. "All the more reason not to pursue him alone." Pausing, he fired a match and lit his cigar. "How do you know where Bixler has gone?"

"He was reported seen in Nuevo Laredo and in Monterrey, heading south with a Mexican man who fits the description of Gilbert Salazar."

"Mmm," said the colonel, drawing smoke. Blowing it out, he went on. "There are a lot of Mexican men to fit that description, but not too many are accompanied by walking oak trees like Wolf Bixler. Especially with one ear practically chewed off."

"You're right there," agreed Jarrell. "There's no mistaking Wolf." Adjusting himself in the chair, he said,

"So anyhow, sir, I figure a lone rider is less conspicuous than a group."

"But let's say you find Bixler; what then? Aren't you also obligated to bring back Salazar?"

"To answer your second question first, sir, no, I'm not obligated to apprehend Salazar. I will if I can, but he didn't kill an officer of the United States Army. Bixler did. To answer your first question, I can handle Bixler."

"You sound mighty sure of that."

"It's my job, Colonel. I can bring him in."

Colonel Barber pulled on his cigar again and said, "You'd better make fast tracks. I assume you know about the political trouble in Mexico."

"Yes, sir," replied the lawman. "They briefed me on it in Austin. President Grant has said that if Porfirio Díaz overthrows President Tejada's government, relations would change between the U.S. and Mexico."

"No question about it," commented Barber. "One of the first things to go would be the extradition pact. Díaz would revoke it for sure. It's not looking good south of the border. You'd better hurry."

Rising to his feet, Jarrell said, "Well, I've taken up enough of your time, sir." Extending his hand, he added, "Save a cell for Bixler. I'm bringing him back."

Shaking the young marshal's hand, Barber said, "Good luck, Stu. Going after the Wolf, you're going to need it."

Jarrell left the post and returned to Waco. He stopped at the Lone Star office and booked himself on the San Antonio stage for the next day. San Antonio was the end of the line for the stagecoach, and he would have to buy a horse there to ride south into Mexico.

The federal marshal tied up some loose ends, leaving his visit at the Garner home till last.

At five o'clock, Jarrell knocked on the door at 224 Poplar Street. Mrs. Garner opened the door. Smiling, but obviously nervous, she said, "Stu! I'm glad you're back. Please come in. I'll tell Peggy you're here."

The woman disappeared and was replaced by Robert Garner, Peggy's father, who entered from the kitchen. Shaking Jarrell's hand, Garner eyed the badge on his vest and said, "So you're going ahead with this law-man's career, eh?"

"Yes, sir." Jarrell nodded.

"I think it's fine, son," the man said, tight-lipped, "but that daughter of mine . . . well, that's another story."

Jarrell did not comment, for Peggy had entered the room. She was a pretty young woman, with a fresh-scrubbed look and long brown hair that fell almost to her slender waistline. She looked at the tall man holding his hat in his hands.

"Hello, Stu," she said quietly.

"Hello," he replied.

"Well, Mother," Garner said to his wife, who had followed Peggy into the room, "these two lovebirds will want the parlor. Let's you and I vacate to the kitchen."

As the middle-aged couple passed from view, Jarrell laid his hat on the table. He turned to find Peggy glaring at his badge.

"I thought you were going to meet me at the stage office," he said plaintively. "Did you forget I was coming in today?"

Peggy turned her back, pretending to adjust something on a knickknack shelf. "No, I didn't forget," she said over her shoulder. "I just figured you had your badge. You didn't need me."

Stuart Jarrell had known it was going to come to this. Peggy had expressed her wishes in no uncertain terms: She did not want to marry a lawman.

Stepping up close behind her, he laid both hands on her shoulders. Peggy's body stiffened.

"Hey," he whispered, "I've been gone for nearly a month. Aren't you glad to see me?"

Still facing away from him, she said, "Of course I'm glad to see you."

Jarrell reached down and lifted her long tresses to his nose. "Mmm," he hummed. "Smells like fresh lilacs. You just wash it?"

She nodded silently.

He kissed the top of her head. "Did you miss me?"

"Yes."

"And you're really glad I'm back?"

"I said I was."

"Well, where's my kiss?"

Peggy held her position for a moment and then slowly turned to face him. The tall man folded her gently into his arms and brought his lips down on hers.

But Peggy's kiss was reserved, her lips stiff. Almost cold. When Jarrell opened his eyes, she was staring at him.

Immediately releasing her, he took a deep breath and let it out slowly through his nose. "That was a little cold," he said in a frustrated tone.

"Maybe you ought to kiss your badge," she said, each word falling like chipped ice.

Stuart Jarrell sighed, raised his arms straight out from his body and then dropped them, slapping the palms of his hands against his legs. Pivoting, he took three steps and then turned around to face her. "You're the first woman I ever heard of who was jealous of a badge," he said, lips pulled tight. "Would you feel better if I wore it on my hat instead of on my chest?"

"I don't want you to wear it at all!" Peggy said heatedly. Her bitter gaze cut across the distance between them. "I will not marry you as long as you wear a badge, Stu!"

"You took that engagement ring when I was wearing a badge," he retorted.

"I still had high hopes when you were marshal of Waco that you would come to your senses and get a decent job."

"What's indecent about being a lawman?" Jarrell stabbed back. "*Somebody* has to keep the peace!"

"Well, let *somebody* do it, then," Peggy snapped, folding her arms across her chest. "Why does it have to be you?"

"It doesn't have to be me, Peggy," Jarrell said, moving a step closer to her. "I want it to be me!"

Pursing her lips into a pout, she said, "If you really love me, you'll forget this lawman thing and find another way to make a living."

"If you really love me, you'll marry me no matter what I do for a living," he countered.

Peggy said nothing, pinning him with a hard glare.

Jarrell looked at her for a moment, his lean, angular face grave and reflective. Licking his dry lips, he said, "Peg, I'm good at what I do, and I enjoy it. I was born to be a lawman. The frontier needs good lawmen to keep the peace."

Not batting an eye, Peggy held her stubborn glare.

"Besides," Jarrell continued, "how many men only twenty-eight years old get an appointment as a United States marshal? Peg, do you realize that most federal marshals are over forty? I know of only one that is thirty-four. Doesn't that mean anything to you?"

Peggy answered sullenly, "Yes. It means you'll die younger."

"Aw, Peg, why do you have to see the dark side of everything?"

"Are you going to tell me the job isn't dangerous? What woman wants to send her husband out the door and wonder if there's some killer out there who's going to make her a widow that day?"

"But Peg—"

"But Peg, nothing!" she blurted. "I am not going to live that way! You can be married to me or to that badge, but not both."

Stuart Jarrell studied the determination in Peggy's eyes. Making one more try, he said, "I met at least fifteen U.S. marshals when I was in Austin. I only remember one who was not married."

"So what?"

"So there are women in this world who are married to United States marshals."

"Well, Peggy Garner is not one of them, and she never will be!"

Jarrell bit his tongue. What he was about to say would not help matters at all.

In a lighter tone, she said, "There is a clerk's job open at Webber's Mercantile. Whoever takes it will probably be a partner in the business someday."

Jarrell looked at her in silence.

"Mr. Emery is looking for a man to train on the printing press at the *Waco Sentinel*. It's good steady work. There will always be newspapers."

More silence.

"Charlie Yates is looking for a potential partner at the feed lot."

There was sadness in Stuart Jarrell's eyes when he spoke. "Peggy, those kind of occupations are not for me. I've got to make a contribution to my fellow man. Making the frontier a safer place to live is my way of doing it."

"Well, you'll do it without me!" Peggy announced icily, pulling off her engagement ring and throwing it at him. It hit him on the left shoulder, bounced to the floor, and slid under a large horsehair sofa.

Jarrell picked up his hat, clapped it on his head, and headed for the door. Without turning around he said, "You're exactly right, Miss Garner, I *will* do it without you!" He slammed the door behind him.

He was almost to the street when he heard the door open. Peggy stomped onto the porch, her face fiery red. She shouted at the top of her lungs, "I'll be waiting, Stuart! You'll be back! But when you come, you'll have to *crawl*, do you hear me? You'll be back, but you'll come back on my terms! I'll be waiting! Do you hear me?"

Her voice penetrated the air long after Jarrell had passed from sight.

Chapter Six

Icy sweat glinted on Wolf Bixler's forehead as José Villa swore and jerked the gallows lever several times.

The trapdoor refused to open.

Prison personnel and inmates looked on in bewilderment, frozen in their places. Agony was imprinted on Wolf's sallow cheeks, and his heart was pounding. The cold sweat began to run into his eyes.

Villa worked the lever another time and then looked helplessly at César Ramos. "I am sorry, Warden. I thought it was fixed."

Ramos swore, swinging a fist through the air. Lifting his eyes to Wolf Bixler, he commanded Villa to remove the noose and return the prisoner to the cell.

José Villa hurried up the stairs and took the scratchy rope from Wolf's neck. "Come, señor," he said to the big man.

Wolf descended the creaky stairs on weak knees. As he reached solid ground, the dark-skinned warden scowled at Villa and said sharply, "I want you to find the problem and repair it. And this time, I mean you repair it! The execution is postponed until sunrise tomorrow."

Four guards ushered a shaky Wolf Bixler to his cell, where his hands were once more shackled in front of him. He sagged onto the bunk as the lock rattled and the guards walked away.

Wolf's shirt was literally soaked with sweat. He palmed

perspiration from his face, wishing his ordeal were over. He did not relish climbing those gallows stairs again.

Ten minutes later, a guard came with a full tray of breakfast. Wolf's stomach was riding the edge of nausea. He told the guard that he could not eat.

When the lock rattled and the guard's footsteps died away, the condemned man lay down on the bunk, his body drained of strength. He felt slightly dizzy. He had looked Death in the face many times, but he had never been through an ordeal like this.

Wolf shuddered as he thought of the sound of that lever being tripped. In the morning he would have to go through the whole thing again, only then there would be no malfunction. He would die for certain at sunrise tomorrow.

An hour had passed when he heard the footsteps of two men coming down the corridor. A key was fitted into the lock and turned, and the door opened. Warden César Ramos entered the cell. The door shut behind him, and the lock rattled again. The footsteps of the guard faded away.

"I want to talk to you, señor," Ramos said, looking down on him.

Wolf eyed him balefully, saying nothing.

"What was it like, Bixler?" asked the dark-skinned man. "It must have been a horrible thing to stand there on the gallows with the rope around your neck, waiting for the trapdoor to drop."

Wolf could not believe what he was hearing. Swinging around and dropping his feet on the floor to the rattle of the chain, he scowled at the Mexican and said, "You sadistic scum. You enjoyed watchin' me go through that, didn't you? What kind of an animal are you?"

Ramos broke into a smile. "Now, now, señor," he said, waggling his finger at the big man, "that is no way for you to talk to the man who saved your life."

Bixler's features darkened. Standing up, he looked down at Ramos, shaking the chain on his wrists in his face. "You've got a lot of nerve comin' in here alone with me! I can crush you with these two hands!"

The warden did not flinch.

Wolf looked at him with speculation. "What do you mean, the man who saved my life?"

Ramos replied levelly, "The trapdoor did not function properly because it was not supposed to. I had José Villa see to it that it was nailed shut."

Wolf stared at him, dumbfounded.

"I wanted you to experience standing on the trapdoor in a cold sweat and hearing the lever tripped," said the Mexican, looking straight into the huge man's questioning eyes. "You are scheduled to go back to the gallows tomorrow morning. Next time, the trapdoor will fall. I guarantee it." Ramos paused for effect and then spoke again. "But there is a way you can miss it altogether."

Wolf looked down at César Ramos in consternation, as if his ears were playing tricks on him. "Am I hearing you right?" he asked, scratching his head.

"Sí," answered Ramos. "I have been authorized by El Presidente Sebastian Lerdo de Tejada to offer you a proposition."

"Wait a minute," Wolf said, shaking his head. "How does your president know me?"

"Do you know a man named William Edwards?"

"I know a Bill Edwards who used to be the marshal at Del Rio, Texas. I broke out of his jail three times."

"Sí," agreed Ramos. "That would be him. He now lives here in Mexico City. He is a close friend of El Presidente."

"I had heard he was no longer in Del Rio, but I didn't know what happened to him."

"Señor Edwards learned about the incident you had with the Salazar brothers and of your trial and pending execution. He is the one who told us of your reputation for jailbreaking. It was because of what he said that we put you in leg irons and kept your wrists in chains."

"What has this got to do with the president?"

"Last night there was an assassination attempt on El Presidente Tejada," replied Ramos. "He—"

The warden's words were interrupted by a pounding noise coming from outside. He stepped to the window and looked out. Turning back, he said, "It is José Villa and my cousin, Arturo Ramos. They are seeing to the trapdoor." Ramos rubbed his temples. "Now, where was I?"

"The assassination attempt," offered the prisoner.

"Oh. Sí. You have heard of the revolution led by Porfirio Díaz?"

"Yes. The Salazar brothers were Díaz's men."

The warden's eyebrows went up. "Oh? They told you that?"

"Sure did. Figured it wouldn't hurt if I knew, since they were going to kill me."

Ramos shook his head. "It is the same all over Mexico. We do not know whom to trust anymore."

"You were telling me about the assassination attempt."

"Sí." Ramos nodded. "There was much shooting. El Presidente was wounded slightly, but his wife, married daughter, and son-in-law were killed."

Wolf waited for Ramos to continue.

"El Presidente knows the assassins will try again," said Ramos. "This Díaz is one mean hombre. He is determined to take over the country. Tejada has another daughter, Rosa. She is twenty years of age. He also has a son, Armand, who is fifteen. Díaz's killers have orders to kill them also."

"How do you know this?" Wolf asked.

"Two of the assassins were shot down by El Presidente's bodyguards during the shooting. One was killed instantly. The other lived long enough to boast that Díaz had ordered the deaths of all members of the Tejada family. This is where your proposition comes in."

"I'm listening."

"El Presidente is going to flee to Acapulco. He knows the revolutionaries will be after him, so he must send his children in another direction for their safety. They must leave this country. As long as Rosa and Armand remain in Mexico, their lives will be in danger."

Wolf Bixler shifted his position, rattling the chain, and said, "What has all this got to do with me?"

"William Edwards, knowing the situation, has told El Presidente of your reputation," explained Ramos. "Tejada has been made aware of your background with the

Comanches and of your amazing prison breaks and your cunning intelligence in eluding lawmen." The warden stopped to chuckle.

"What's funny?" asked Wolf.

"This Señor Edwards," Ramos remarked. "Though you have given him much trouble in the past, he admires you."

"You don't say."

"Sí. He says that you are rough, tough, and very resourceful. That you are quite expert at surviving in wilderness country. He says the thing he admires most about you is that you are a man of your word. Señor Edwards says you would die before you would go back on your word."

"Among the Comanche people there is nothing but contempt for a man who breaks his word," Wolf explained. "Whites are double-tongued. Mexicans, too."

The warden cleared his throat. "I cannot blame you for how you feel. I heard about your testimony in court of how Gilbert Salazar tricked you. May I proceed with the proposition?"

"Please do."

"It is simply this. If you want to evade the gallows, you must agree to take Rosa and Armand north into Texas. You must get them away from Díaz's assassins."

"Go on."

"If you agree to do it, I will arrange for your escape before morning."

Wolf looked at him quizzically. "Escape? Why do I have to escape? If I agree to take these two kids to Texas, why can't you just unlock the gate and turn me loose?"

Shaking his head, Ramos said, "It cannot be done like that, señor. Porfirio Díaz's men have been infiltrating Tejada's government for quite some time. He has spies in many places. We have no way of knowing who or where they are. Some of them could be among the personnel in this prison. That is why your escape must appear to be real."

Ramos continued, "Your reputation for being an expert at jailbreaking is already quite well known throughout the prison. Señor Edwards will see that it is spread through the government offices in Mexico City, once you have escaped. No one will suspect this arrangement. Díaz's men will have no way of knowing that you are leading Tejada's daughter and son to safety."

Wolf nodded.

"You will have to travel the back trails through rough country," the warden explained. "You must keep Rosa and Armand from being seen by people as much as possible."

"I could get lost myself travelin' that way," Wolf commented. "Gilbert and I took the main trails comin' down here."

"That has already been thought of, señor," Ramos said with a smile. "There is a man ready to go with you who knows the back country between here and the Texas border quite well. He will guide you."

Wolf shook his head. "You're a clever man, Ramos. But I have a couple of questions."

"All right."

"What do I do with these two kids when I get them across the Texas border?"

"You proceed to San Antonio," the warden replied. "A man who can be trusted will be waiting for you there. His name is Dido Gomez. You will turn Rosa and Armand over to him. Dido once worked on El Presidente's staff. A message has already been sent by boat up the coast of the Gulf of Mexico. Gomez is being told in the message that Señor Wolf Bixler is coming to San Antonio with Tejada's children."

Wolf regarded César Ramos with a steely look. "You and your president are pretty sure of yourselves, ain't you?"

Ramos grinned. "Shouldn't we be?"

Wolf lifted his shackled hands, using one to rub the back of his neck. "Yeah. I guess so."

"Especially after I let you stand on that trapdoor, listening to the lever snap, eh?"

"Shoosh!" breathed the big man. "You didn't have to go to all that trouble. Just lookin' at that noose swayin' in the wind was enough."

"Actually I had a dual purpose in putting you through it," said Ramos. "One was to let you get a good taste of the gallows so you would not have to think twice when I offered you the proposition. The other was to convince everyone in the prison that we tried to hang you as scheduled."

"In case Díaz has men planted here."

"Sí. There are actually only two men here that I am positive I can trust. One is José Villa. I have no doubt about him."

"And Villa knew the trapdoor was nailed shut all that time," Wolf said in wonderment. "He sure put on a good act!"

Ramos smiled. "He *is* a good hangman. The other man I trust is my cousin, Arturo. He is the guard who nailed the trapdoor shut. Actually, Arturo went out in the middle of the night and tampered with the lever so the guards would see it giving José trouble from the start this morning. This made it believable when the trapdoor did not function later."

Wolf eyed him cautiously and said, "What about that guard I grabbed this morning? You really would have let me kill him, wouldn't you?"

The warden's face flushed even darker. "Sí. There was no way I could let you get away. El Presidente's children must be spared at all costs."

"Warden," said Wolf, "if you can send a message by boat up to Texas, why can't you send Rosa and Armand by boat?"

"That would be too dangerous, señor," Ramos responded. "Díaz's troops will be watching the coastline closely. All boats will be searched."

Wolf looked the warden straight in the eye. "Ramos, let's say that I give you my word that I will do my best to deliver the kids safely to this Gomez. What if I decide to break my word, just this once? What if I abandon those two kids once I'm out of your sight and run away? Have you thought of that?"

César Ramos smiled broadly. "Why are you in this predicament right now?" he asked. "It is because you wanted gold for your Comanche friends, no?"

"You're right," he admitted.

Still smiling, Ramos said, "The reason Dido Gomez left Mexico, señor, was to smuggle gold out of this country and hide it in the United States. It is El Presidente Tejada's personal gold. He saw this Díaz revolution coming nearly a year ago, and just in case he had to leave Mexico, he sent the gold out so he would have money in the United States. Once he knows Rosa and Armand are safe, he plans to make his way to San Antonio himself. Dido has the gold. His instructions are to give you twenty thousand dollars in gold when you turn Rosa and Armand over to him."

Wolf sighed and said, "How do I know this deal won't be like the one Gilbert Salazar handed me?"

"You don't," replied Ramos flatly. "But because I may be telling you the truth, you will not abandon the young Tejadas. You will escort them safely to Gomez. The chance that the gold might really be there will drive you. You have everything to gain by making the attempt. The alternative is the gallows tomorrow morning."

"I have to give you credit," Wolf remarked, rubbing his bearded jaw. "You've given me little choice."

"You might say that." Ramos grinned. "Now, are you aware that it is over eight hundred miles from here to San Antonio? It is winter. Many dangers lurk in the rugged country ahead of you. There is the possibility that the assassins may learn of your flight in spite of all that we do to keep it a secret. Also, there is the absolute certainty that you will be pursued by the Federales, simply because you have escaped from this prison."

Wolf Bixler breathed deeply. "You're just full of happy thoughts, ain't you, Ramos? Do you know what the odds are that I'll get those kids to San Antonio?"

"Slim, at best," acknowledged the warden. "But if there is a man on earth who can do it, Wolf Bixler, you are he. It beats the alternative, though, does it not?"

"Can't argue with that," the big man said resignedly. "All right. How do we work this escape?"

Ramos produced a pocket watch, studied it for a

moment, and then said, "I told the guard to come for me in thirty minutes. We still have about fifteen."

"What does he think you're doin' in here all this time?" queried Wolf.

Ramos shrugged his shoulders, throwing palms upward. "I am known as a tender-hearted and compassionate man, señor. So I have come to console the poor soul who suffered severely this morning because of a malfunctioning trapdoor."

"Didn't anyone wonder why you would come in here alone with me?"

"It is not uncommon for me to talk to a prisoner alone," answered Ramos. "Armed guards are not so far away. Besides, it makes me look brave and courageous."

Wolf shook his head.

Pulling out a pencil and small pad of paper, Ramos said, "I need you to tell me what you want in the way of weapons and equipment."

Wolf thought a moment and then said, "Needless to say, we'll need a horse for each person. Better get me a big one."

"I understand."

"Let's see . . . we'll also need a packhorse, and we'll need all the food it can carry. Canteens. Matches. Bedrolls. I want the kids each to have a revolver and holster. Nothing smaller than thirty-eight caliber. The guide should have a rifle and revolver. I want two Navy Colt forty-fives with holsters, a rifle, and a good-sized hunting knife. Give me at least a hundred rounds of ammunition for each gun. Oh, yes—bring me a couple of bandoliers loaded with forty-fives for my Colts."

Ramos scribbled it all down. "All right," he said. "Now let's talk about getting you out of here."

Checking his watch again, César Ramos said, "We have about ten minutes. You understand the guard is not in on this. He will have to be subdued."

"Okay," Wolf replied. "I assume you are to be my hostage. What do you want me to do?"

Ramos grinned. "If you were planning a break, what would you do?"

"Well . . ." Wolf thought for a few moments. "I usu-

ally plan them out carefully beforehand, but there isn't
time for that. I'll have to act on the spur of the moment. Can I hurt the guard much?"

"Do whatever it takes to get us out of here."

"What do we do when we get out?"

"Of the cell or of the prison?"

"The prison, Ramos," said Wolf blandly. "I can get us
out, but what happens when we get outside?"

"We will have to . . . how is it they say in your
country? *Play it by ear*. I will lead you to the place
where Rosa and Armand are being kept. It is about
twenty miles from here, in the mountains."

"We'll need a couple of horses right away," Wolf
said.

"The stables are outside the walls on the west side."

"All right." Wolf's mind was working fast. "I'm going
to lie down on the floor. You tell the guard that what I
went through at the gallows was too much for me. I was
in terrible shape when you found me on the bunk. I got
up babbling and then fell on the floor. Ask him to help
you pick me up and put me back on the bunk. Tell him
you will have to call a doctor. Be sure you take my
ankles. Let him reach for my top end."

"All right." Ramos nodded.

"Has he got a key to my irons?"

"Yes. He has door keys. Any man who has door keys
has one on his ring."

They heard a door unlatch down at the end of the
corridor.

"He's coming!" Ramos whispered. "Bixler . . ."

"Yes?" Wolf said as he brushed away two cockroaches
and lay on his back in the middle of the floor.

"If you have to hurt me to make this look real, do it."

Wolf looked up at him with admiration. "You're really dedicated to Tejada, ain't you?"

"Completely," came the reply.

Chapter Seven

The guard tapped on the door, saying, "Señor Warden, I am here to let you out."

"We have a problem, Gallegos," replied Ramos, raising his voice. "Come in."

Gallegos opened the door to find the warden down on one knee, bending over Wolf Bixler, whose eyes were closed.

"What is the matter?" asked Gallegos, bending low to look into the prisoner's face.

"I don't know," replied the warden. "I think that situation on the gallows was too much for him. He was lying on the bunk mumbling incoherently when I came into the cell. When I tried to talk to him, he looked at me in a strange way. He got up off the bunk and began babbling like his mind had snapped. He paced back and forth in here for some time, and I could not get him to even acknowledge that I was in the cell. Then suddenly he collapsed. He has been unconscious for several minutes."

"Should I get the doctor?" asked the guard.

"I think you should," said Ramos, "but first help me get him on the bunk."

As he spoke, Ramos moved toward Wolf's feet, forcing Gallegos to take the other end. As Gallegos bent down to grip the big man under the arms, Wolf unleashed both fists in a savage punch, connecting with the guard's left jaw.

Gallegos flipped backward from the force of the double-fisted blow and hit the floor hard. He was dazed, but still conscious. Shaking his head, he rolled to his knees and tried to focus on Wolf, who was now standing over him.

Again Wolf swung, slugging the guard solidly. Gallegos went down, unconscious. Within seconds, Wolf had pulled the revolver from the guard's holster and unloaded it while Ramos freed him of the leg irons and shackles with Gallegos's keys.

Wolf then pulled the unconscious man's shirt off and tore from it a long strip, which he used to bind Ramos's wrists behind his back. "When we walk out of here, I'll be holdin' this revolver at your head. They'll know that by shooting me, they'll kill you."

Gallegos was beginning to stir. Wolf let the guard regain consciousness and clear his head. Gallegos immediately saw the dangerous position of the warden. Wolf had the hammer eared back and the muzzle under Ramos's left jaw, pointing upward. A bullet entering his head at that angle would rip through the brain.

"Now, Gallegos," Wolf said with gravel in his voice, "I'm going to give you five minutes to spread the word to all the guards. You'd better see that every one of them has the picture. If I get shot, your warden dies."

For a moment, Gallegos stood by the cell door as though carved out of wood. Finally he worked his tongue loose and said to Ramos, "I will see that they all understand, Warden."

"And be sure they know not to follow us, Gallegos," Wolf said threateningly. "If I see hide or hair of any guards, I'll kill Ramos."

The guard nodded nervously and hastened down the corridor.

When five minutes had passed, Wolf said, "All right, Warden, let's go. Put a frightened look on your face and keep it there. I'm dependin' on you leadin' me out of here to the stables. We'll take two horses and turn the rest of them loose. It'll take the guards a while to run the horses down so they can pursue us."

The two men made their way down the corridor to

the door. Flinging it open with his free hand, Wolf shouted, "All right, all of you! We're comin' out! If you want your warden to live, you'd better not take one shot in my direction! Remember, I've got nothin' to lose!"

Slowly they inched their way down the stone steps, the gun muzzle held tight against Ramos's jaw. Once in the courtyard, they saw the guards positioned along the top of the walls, rifles held loosely in their hands. Those in the tower let their guns rest in the crooks of their arms.

The entire complex was dead quiet. Prisoners watched with interest from their barred windows, and José Villa and Arturo Ramos looked on from beside the gallows. Two guards stood by the gate, and one of them swung it open. Wolf gave them a contemptuous sneer as he inched the warden past them. Ramos let them see trepidation in his eyes.

When they were outside the wall, Wolf said to the guard, "Close the gate!" He looked up at the guards at the top of the wall. They were keeping a close eye on them.

It was fifty yards from the west gate to the corral fence where a dozen horses were kept. No one was near the stable. As they passed from view of the guards, Wolf said, "We'll have to work fast, Ramos. They'll follow, as sure as anything."

Within moments, the two men had each saddled a horse. Wolf took the bullets from his pocket and loaded the revolver. "We'll lead your horse and both ride mine," he said. "I'll hold the gun to your head till we're away from here."

Swinging the corral gate open, he drove the other horses out, waving his arms and shouting at them. He and the warden quickly mounted the larger horse, Wolf seated behind Ramos with the muzzle at the base of his skull. They rode out, leading the other horse.

Wolf spurred the horse on but reined it in when he spotted two guards behind some bushes outside the walls. "Hey, you two!" he bellowed. "Throw down your guns and get back inside those walls!"

"Do what he says!" Ramos called out. "He will kill me!"

The two guards dropped their weapons and began to walk slowly toward the west gate. Wolf swung the revolver around and fired, sending a bullet into the dirt near their heels. Instantly the two men broke into a run and darted from view.

Wolf spurred the horse to a trot. He was pleased to see that the other horses had scattered well. It would take the guards a good while to round them up.

Half a mile from the prison, Ramos mounted the second horse, and the two men galloped eastward into the mountains, the warden in the lead.

The jagged peaks of the majestic eastern range of the Sierra Madres loomed before them, bold and high. Soon they were weaving among huge rocks and boulders, evergreens and white-barked birch trees towering above them. Gaining altitude, they stopped periodically and let the horses rest.

After two hours, Wolf and Ramos pulled into a ravine and dismounted.

"I think it is best that we wait here until dark," said Ramos. "We have been on hard surface some of the time, but we have left some tracks on the soft spots. The cabin where Rosa and Armand are being kept is about three miles due south of here. I do not want to lead our pursuers in that direction. Rather than work at covering our tracks, we will wait in this ravine."

While the sun crept slowly across the sky, Wolf Bixler sat on a rock and pondered the journey before him. It would be quite an undertaking—nursemaiding a couple of Mexican kids through eight hundred miles of wilderness, dodging Federales, assassins, and who knew what else.

Wolf was never comfortable around children. They made him edgy and nervous. He reminded himself that Tejada's children were not small. Rosa was twenty, and she would be past the whiny stage. But Armand was only fifteen, that awkward period of changing from a boy into a young man. This journey would no doubt be tough on him; it was sure to mature him beyond his years.

Wolf thought of the gold Ramos said would be his at the end of the journey. Somehow he had a deep-seated confidence that the man was telling him the truth. He hoped that Chief Iron Face and his Comanche warriors could withstand the white man's army a little longer. Soon there would be plenty of rifles and sufficient ammunition.

He looked up and checked the position of the sun. *Must be about noon,* he thought.

Ramos, sitting on a rock some ten feet away, saw Wolf eye the sun, and he pulled out his watch. "It is ten minutes before twelve, señor."

Wolf laid a hand on his stomach, hunger claiming his attention. "I hope you've got some food at that cabin," he said to the warden.

César Ramos smiled. "There will be plenty to fill you tonight."

The two horses were ground reined some twenty yards away in the rocky ravine. Suddenly, one of them lifted its head and nickered, and the other one followed suit.

Wolf jumped to his feet. "Someone's comin'," he said.

Both men stood listening. At first they heard only the sound of the breeze in the treetops. Then came a faint rumble that sounded like distant thunder, and within half a minute the sound of galloping horses was distinguishable.

West of the draw was an open meadow that extended half a mile to a thick forest. Both men peered in that direction, from where the horses were approaching, and waited. Soon they saw six prison guards pushing shiny, lathered horses as fast as they could go.

Wolf and Ramos moved cautiously to their own animals and stroked them reassuringly to keep them from making any noise. The riders disappeared into the dense woods above and soon could no longer be heard.

"They may come back this way," observed Ramos.

"It is best that we remain here until after dark and then proceed to the cabin."

As they sat down again on their respective rocks, César Ramos looked at his companion and said, "I must tell you where to find Dido Gomez when you get to San Antonio."

"Oh, yeah." Wolf grunted. "I meant to ask you about that."

"I assume you have been in San Antonio."

"Many times," Wolf confirmed. "They have one of the more comfortable jails in Texas."

The dark-skinned warden smiled. "No doubt you have seen the old Franciscan mission in San Antonio."

"The Alamo?"

"Sí."

"Yeah. Sits right close to the San Antonio River. Lot of blood was spilled there back in thirty-six. A good deal of it was Mexican blood, they tell me."

Ramos nodded, "Sí. Those North Americans are tough hombres."

"Nobody bothers with the old Alamo anymore," said Wolf. "It just stands there in the wind and the rain."

"That is where you are to meet Dido Gomez," Ramos said. "He will be waiting inside the chapel building. You are to turn Rosa and Armand over to him there. He will make the arrangements at that time to give you the twenty thousand in gold."

"He won't have it with him?"

"Not at the Alamo. It is hidden in the hills to the north of San Antonio, I understand."

"Okay." Wolf nodded. All was quiet for a moment, and then he said, "Exactly what are you going to do after the kids and that guide and I take off?"

"I will take the horse you are now riding and lead it behind mine, heading straight south of Mexico City and leaving two sets of tracks for a good distance. When I find a spot where the ground is hard and a horse cannot be tracked, I will make myself look like you hit me on the head and rode away. Someone then will find me with these two horses. I will tell him that you stole another horse and that I think you were heading on southward for Guatemala. This will throw off the Federales."

"I hope you get away with it," said Wolf. "Things could get sticky for you if anyone figures you helped me to escape."

"They won't." Ramos grinned.

The afternoon passed slowly, but finally the sun went down. They had seen no more sign of the prison guards. As darkness began to blanket the mountains, the two men mounted up.

"I will take you to the cabin and introduce you to Rosa and Armand, señor," Ramos said, settling in the saddle. "Then I will ride to the city to gather the weapons and equipment you have requested. It will take the better part of the night for me to do this, but I will be back before dawn so you can be on your way by sunrise."

Under cover of darkness the two men wound their way to a remote mountainside, where a two-room cabin was wedged into the steep slope. Thin wisps of smoke trailed toward the black, star-spangled sky from a stove-pipe chimney protruding through the roof. From curtained windows came yellow light, forming slanted rectangular shapes on the ground.

Wolf noticed a small barn nearby and several horses in the surrounding corral. "Looks like you've got more than enough horses stashed here already," he said to Ramos as they drew near the cabin.

"I figured El Presidente might have already taken care of that," said the warden. "I hope you will find a stout one to fit your need."

As they were dismounting, a window curtain swept back and a swarthy face appeared and then was gone. The door opened and a dark figure stood silhouetted against the lantern light inside. The figure spoke. "Ah, César! I am glad that you made it!"

Ramos ejected a coarse laugh. "I tell you, Pedro. This Wolf Bixler is an expert. He got us out without a hitch!"

Pedro Llamas was a short, thick-bodied man with

mahogany skin, a broad nose, and yellow teeth that were chipped, broken, and quite crooked.

"Wolf Bixler," said Ramos, as the two men stepped onto the porch, "shake hands with Pedro Llamas. He is to be your guide. Knows the country like he knows the back of his hand."

Llamas's stubby hand was lost in Wolf's fist as they briefly shook.

"Rosa and the boy are inside," Llamas said to the warden, turning and moving through the door.

Ramos followed, and Wolf brought up the rear, ducking his head as he entered. The two-room cabin seemed to shrink in size with Wolf's massive frame in it.

The smell of food cooking brought saliva to the big man's mouth. Pedro stepped toward a small table near the stove, where Rosa and Armand Tejada were seated. "Rosa, Armand . . ." he said, gesturing toward the smaller man, "this is Warden César Ramos from the federal prison."

Both young people smiled past the fear in their eyes, and their gaze lifted to the newcomer, whose head nearly touched the ceiling.

Dipping his head in a slight bow, Ramos said, "Please accept my condolences on the loss of your dear mother and your sister and brother-in-law."

"Gracias," replied Rosa, glancing at Ramos as she spoke and then looking back to Wolf.

"Gracias, señor," repeated Armand.

"I want you to know," Ramos stated emphatically, "that my loyalty is with your father. Therefore, your safety is of my utmost concern."

"Gracias," they responded in unison.

"Because of this," continued the warden, "I have brought you a man who is going to take you to San Antonio, where you will be safe from Díaz's wicked men." Motioning for the towering American to come close, he said, "I want you to meet Señor Wolf Bixler."

Stepping to the table, Wolf looked down on them with his sober face and said, "It is a long way to San Antonio, my young friends, but between Pedro and myself, we will deliver you to Dido Gomez safe and sound."

Rosa and Armand were overwhelmed with Wolf Bixler's awesome size. They both nodded and smiled weakly, but neither spoke.

César Ramos suggested they eat. He needed to be going soon, so he could be back with the weapons and supplies by dawn.

During the meal, Wolf observed the young Mexicans carefully. Rosa was small of body, yet well proportioned and mature for twenty years. When she was standing, Wolf judged her to be just an inch or two over five feet. She was not as dark complected as her brother, and her skin was smooth and silky with a creamy texture. Her features looked as if they were hand carved by a sculptor with a keen eye for beauty. She had full lips, even, white teeth, and large dark-brown eyes that accentuated her cream-colored complexion. Her long, black hair reflected the dancing light of the lantern that hung over the table.

The beautiful young woman picked absently at her supper, a melancholy cast to her face. Wolf understood. Rosa's whole world had just been shattered with the sudden, violent death of her mother, sister, and brother-in-law. Her father was deposed from the highest office in the land, now a fugitive running for his life. And to top it off, she and her remaining sibling were running for theirs.

Despite this miserable situation, twice, as Wolf let his dark eyes fall on Rosa's face, she gave him a soft smile. But neither time did he return it. He had forgotten how to smile. The years with hateful, greedy white men had turned him sour, filling his heart with bitterness. Wolf Bixler could not remember the last time he had smiled, much less laughed.

His eyes strayed to Armand. The youth was a couple of inches taller than his sister, slight of build, and a bit awkward at this transitional period in his life. His eyes were the color of his sister's, and his curly hair was thick and coal black. Wolf could see that someday he would be a handsome man.

César Ramos finished eating first. Rising from the table, he said, "I will be on my way now. I will return by dawn." Looking at Wolf, he added, "You will like Pedro, Señor Wolf. He is a close friend to El Presidente and the best guide in Mexico. He is good with a gun. I am sure you two will be an excellent team."

After Wolf nodded his assent, Ramos strode to the door, pulled it open, and then spoke again to the big man. "Try to get some sleep, señor. You have had a hard day. I doubt that you slept any last night."

Wolf nodded again. The warden stepped out and closed the door.

"We had all better get some sleep," Pedro Llamas said, pushing back from the table.

Armand helped Rosa clear the table and wash the dishes while Wolf and Pedro Llamas stretched out on the floor to sleep.

When the brother and sister were finished, they stood over Wolf Bixler, looking down at his huge frame.

"He scares me, Armand," whispered Rosa. "He's so big and rough. He seems to be angry with the whole world."

Armand poked his sister, grinned, and whispered back, "You do not understand him, Rosa. If you did, you would not be afraid of him. He is simply a strong, rugged man. Just like I want to be some day!"

Chapter Eight

Just before dawn, everyone in the cabin was awakened by the sound of a wagon rattling into the yard. A horse whinnied and blew.

Rosa rolled from her cot and fired a lantern. Crossing the room, she lit another.

Wolf Bixler sat up, yawned, stretched his arms, and rose to his feet. Armand and Pedro were rubbing sleep from their eyes when the door came open.

Wolf's jaw sagged in puzzlement when a skinny Mexican man came through the door carrying a small black-haired girl, who was just waking up.

"Good morning, Diego." Smiling, Rosa moved toward the newcomers with outstretched hands. "Let me have her. How is Father?"

"Your father's wound, it is not bad at all, Rosa," replied the little man, handing the child to her. "He left the city immediately after we picked up Josefina."

At this point, Diego's eyes found the hulking frame of Wolf Bixler.

"Oh," said Rosa, cuddling Josefina, "Diego, I want you to meet Señor Wolf Bixler. Señor Bixler, this is a very close friend of our family, Diego Corral."

Diego shook hands with the big man.

"And this sleepy little girl," Rosa said to Wolf, "is my niece, Josefina Montoya."

Wolf's face stiffened. "What's she doing here?" he asked with an edge of gruffness in his voice.

Rosa looked at him quizzically as Josefina laid her head on her shoulder and went back to sleep. "She is going to San Antonio with us. Did not Señor Ramos tell you?"

"No, he did not!" Wolf growled, heading for the door.

Stepping off the porch, he stomped to where César Ramos was unhitching the team from the wagon. "Ramos!" he bellowed. "You didn't tell me anything about a little girl going on this trip!"

"Oh, didn't I?" said the warden without turning around. "It must have slipped my mind."

"Look," breathed the big man, "it's going to be hard enough gettin' four people to San Antonio, but—"

"Six," cut in Ramos, turning to face him in the dull light from the cabin.

"Six?"

"Diego Corral is going along, also."

Wolf swore, pivoting in a half circle, placing his hands on his hips, and then completing the circle. "Why do either one of them have to go?" he demanded. "Children are a problem and a nuisance. She can't be more than four years old!"

"Josefina is six," Ramos said calmly. "She is El Presidente's granddaughter. It was her parents who were killed along with Señora Tejada. El Presidente is the most vulnerable to attack, and Josefina would be in grave danger traveling with him. She has no other family, and so she must stay with Rosa and Armand."

Wolf sighed. "And Diego? He's forty-five if he's a day. He can't be Tejada's grandson. Why is he going along?"

"Diego is a very close friend of the Tejada family. He was their gardener. Josefina has loved him and trusted him since she was very small. He has come along to care for her. This way she will be less of a problem and a nuisance to you. She calls him uncle."

Wolf looked toward the saw-toothed mountains eastward, now silhouetted against a graying sky. Turning back to Ramos, he growled, "Have you got any more surprises for me?"

"Cool down, my friend," Ramos said softly. "Are you forgetting what would be happening to you this morning if you had not agreed to go on this journey? Between Rosa and Diego, the child will be taken care of."

As Wolf was digesting what Ramos had just said, the warden went on to explain that the message sent by boat to Dido Gomez had gone before Tejada decided to send Josefina and Diego to San Antonio. Gomez would not know about them, but it would be no problem.

Wolf swore under his breath. He was stuck with the situation.

César Ramos assigned Armand Tejada to finish unharnessing the team and put them in the corral. He was then to halter the packhorse and bring it to the cabin. The men carried the weapons, ammunition, food, and supplies into the cabin, along with some clothing for Wolf.

Rosa was cooking breakfast and had coffee going. While the men stuffed ammunition in their saddlebags and strapped on their weapons, she packed food in burlap sacks. Josefina was asleep on a cot in a corner.

Armand entered and announced that the packhorse was at the porch.

Wolf was sitting at the table, punching .45 caliber cartridges into two bandolier belts. Eyeing Armand, he said, "Hey, boy, you ever fire a revolver?"

"Sí, señor." The black-haired youth nodded. "I am very good, too."

"Armand speaks the truth, Señor Wolf," Diego Corral maintained. "His papa had me teach him and Rosa the proper use of the *pistola*. They are both very good. Of course Rosa is the best because she is so beautiful—the bullets fly straighter for her! Armand . . . well, he is not so beautiful, and the bullets do not care if they please him. They mostly go crooked!"

Rosa looked up to see if Wolf would smile at Diego's attempt at humor. César Ramos laughed, but Wolf's face held its scowl. Rosa and her brother exchanged glances. Diego was looking at Wolf with a broad smile under his heavy mustache, but when the big man's expression did not alter, the smile died on his lips.

Wolf shoved a .38 revolver, a holster, and a box of cartridges across the table toward Armand. "There you are, boy," he said in his deep voice. "Put the revolver on your belt. It's for your protection, so use it if you have to."

Smiling, Armand eagerly picked up the holster and strung it on his belt.

Sliding another set of the exact same items toward Rosa, Wolf said, "Same goes for you, girl. That *is* a belt on your skirt, there, ain't it?"

Rosa was dressed in a pink silk blouse and black, ankle-length wool skirt. The skirt was held to her slender waist by a black belt half an inch in width that matched her low-heeled boots. A bit intimidated by Wolf's brusque manner, she nodded and accepted the gun and accompaniments without speaking.

The big man continued filling the bandoliers with bullets.

Little Josefina awakened and sat up on the cot. No one noticed her until she said, "Good morning, Uncle Diego."

The skinny Mexican smiled broadly, crossed the room, and picked her up. "Good morning to you, Señorita Josefina," he chirped. "Did my little girl get enough sleep?"

"Sí," she answered, rubbing her eyes. Looking toward Rosa, who stood by the stove, she said, "I am hungry."

Rosa rounded the table and moved to Diego and the child. She kissed Josefina's rosy cheek and whispered something in her ear. The child nodded, and Diego lowered her to the floor. Rosa put on a leather jacket, wrapped Josefina in a serape, and led her outside.

Wolf Bixler had gotten his first good look at Josefina Montoya and found she was a beautiful child. Her ink-black eyes were even larger in proportion than her Aunt Rosa's. By the time she was sixteen, she would give her aunt a run for her money on looks, he figured.

After five minutes, Rosa returned with Josefina, who was sporting goosebumps from the chill mountain air.

The little girl ran to Armand and wrapped her arms around his neck. Armand hugged her in return.

Rosa pointed to the stout guide and said, "Josefina, this is Señor Pedro Llamas. He is going to guide us on our trip."

Josefina, a very affectionate and demonstrative child, Wolf thought, now ran to Llamas and reached up to him. He picked her up, saying, "Hello, little muchacha." She hugged his neck.

Rosa looked at Wolf from the corner of her eye. He was loading his two Colt .45 revolvers while observing the scene on the opposite side of the table. She saw a hint of apprehension in his dark eyes and knew what he was fearing.

With a warm sense of felicity suddenly surging through her body, she said, "And Josefina, this big man over here is Señor Wolf Bixler. He is going to protect us on our trip. You should come and give him a love."

Wolf's hard-lined face blanched white as he picked up a holster and slid the revolver into it. He was trapped. Josefina rounded the table, crawled up into his lap, and wrapped her warm, tiny arms around his thick, muscled neck.

Rosa smiled to herself when she saw Wolf's agony. His hands kept hold of the gun and holster, and he made no move to return the child's affection. Rosa thought by the look on his face, a person would think someone had draped a snake around his shoulders.

Josefina, not noticing the big man's lack of warmth toward her, slid to the floor and looked up into his face. She studied him for a moment amd then looked at her aunt and asked, "Rosa, is he what wolfs look like?"

Wolf Bixler gave her a look of disdain.

Rosa smiled and said, "No, honey. That is just his name."

Josefina said, "Oh." Then setting her dark eyes on him, she asked, "Why is your name Wolf, señor?"

"Just because it is, little black-eyed girl," he mumbled.

Rosa had heard William Edwards tell her father of Wolf's reputation. She mentally concurred with his description. Wolf Bixler was a big, tough, crusty man who was a stranger to tenderness or sentimentality. He had no time for little black-eyed girls. She told herself that he would not be quite so intimidating if he were not so huge. She would just have to get used to him, she resolved.

But Wolf Bixler did not intimidate Josefina Montoya. Even with the gruff answer she had just received, she gave him a friendly smile.

The smile began to warm him, and to shake off its effect, he stood up and strapped the holsters on his waist, along with a sheath bearing a nine-inch hunting knife. Then he crisscrossed the bandoliers over his chest. "Let's eat breakfast," he said, running eyes over the group.

While they ate, he talked about the trip. "The rules are simple. Everyone will obey me without any questions. If I tell the group or one of you to do something . . . or *not* to do something . . . you do it, with no argument. My objective is to get us all safely to San Antonio. Gettin' there is yours and my best interest, and I won't forget it. But my decisions are final. Understood?"

"We will all obey you, Señor Wolf," spoke up Rosa. "We know you are experienced in this sort of thing, and we are not."

"Speaking for myself, Wolf," said Armand, "I am glad you are the one taking us to San Antonio. I will do whatever you say."

Rosa cleared her throat. "Armand. Your manners! You will address him as Señor Wolf."

"Sorry," said the youth, dipping his chin.

Flashing Wolf one of his winsome smiles, Diego Corral said, "Señor Wolf, be it known to you and this entire group that I am totally dedicated to El Presidente Sebastian Lerdo de Tejada. I will do all I can to protect his children and his little granddaughter with my very life. You can count on me."

The stocky Pedro Llamas drained his tin cup of strong black coffee and said, "You are our leader, Wolf, but I think we need an understanding about one thing."

Wolf looked at him and said, "And that is?"

"I am the guide. All decisions as to the route we follow will be mine. I know the country well. I have traveled it many times in all seasons of the year."

"I'll agree to that," said Wolf. "Although I do reserve the right to leave it open to discussion between the two of us, should circumstances warrant."

"Something *could* come up that would necessitate a discussion, I suppose," Pedro said. "I agree to that."

"All right," Wolf said, running his gaze among the circle of faces. "We will pull out in half an hour."

Chairs scraped on the floor as each person set about to do what was needed in order to meet the deadline. Pedro would saddle the horses. Diego and Armand would load the packhorse, and Rosa would wash the dishes.

Warden César Ramos bid Rosa and Josefina good-bye and then walked out into the sunrise with Wolf Bixler. Bidding farewell to the men and Armand, he mounted his horse and said to the huge bearded man, "Well, I must ride south and play hostage to a ruthless Wolf Bixler who is headed for Guatemala."

"I just hope the Federales buy it."

Ramos smiled. "One never knows about them. But I will do my best." Extending his hand, he gripped Wolf's and said, "Best of luck, amigo."

Without returning the smile, Wolf quipped, "I never thought I would hear a prison warden call me amigo!"

"Get those kids through to San Antonio," said Ramos, "and you are my friend for life."

With that he wheeled the horse and rode away, leading the other mount they had taken from the prison.

Wolf watched until the warden was swallowed by the forest. Then he turned to see the sky turning yellow above the jagged peaks to the east. He took a deep breath of the cold mountain air and exhaled it in a cloud of vapor. It was good to be alive!

The sun was peeking over the snow-covered mountains when Wolf Bixler and his group mounted up and headed north through the rugged Oriental Range of the Sierra Madres.

Pedro Llamas took the lead as the horses fell into single file. Diego Corral, with Josefina riding double, followed next, with Rosa Tejada third and Armand fourth, leading the packhorse behind his own mount. Wolf Bixler, on a large sorrel gelding, brought up the rear.

They descended some nine hundred feet from the cabin and then leveled off in a narrow valley where the sun would not shine for another hour. The gigantic jaws of the Sierra Madres crowded in upon them, the ancient snowcapped peaks standing tall and proud from their untold centuries of survival.

Talk was minimal, except for Josefina, who chattered intermittently with Diego.

Pedro Llamas led them on a direct course north, though the rocky terrain caused much winding and changing of direction.

Wolf Bixler warned everyone to keep a sharp lookout. The Federales might have sent units in every direction from the prison. There was also the possibility that a spy who had infiltrated Tejada's government would learn of this trek to San Antonio. If so, Díaz's assassins would be on their trail.

Wolf alerted them, too, to the fact that wild animals roamed these mountains. When they stopped to rest, or made camp, no one was to leave the immediate area alone. Another lurking danger were *banditos*.

When Wolf had finished his warning speech, Josefina spoke up and said, "I won't be afraid as long as you are with us, Señor Wolf."

The big man gave her an impassive look and then straightened around in his saddle.

From his place at the rear of the column, Armand Tejada studied the broad back of Wolf Bixler. Every inch of the man spoke of harnessed strength and power. *He is not afraid of anything*, Armand thought with admiration.

When the sun reached its zenith in the blue expanse overhead, Wolf called a halt. They were on a small plateau on the side of a mountain, surrounded by huge boulders and giant trees that seemed to stand as great sentinels over the uneven land.

Sitting in the sunshine to soak up what warmth they could, they ate cold beans and hardtack, washing them down with water from the canteens. Wolf thought it best not to have a fire, since smoke lifting above the treetops would tell any pursuers their exact position.

While they sat in a circle on the ground and ate, a chilly wind swept across the mountain, stealing away the sun's warmth. Rosa fastened the top button of the leather jacket she wore and wrapped herself in the serape hanging loose on her shoulders.

César Ramos had brought Wolf Bixler a sheepskin coat and a broad-brimmed hat, which Wolf had worn until the sun began to put out some heat. He went to his horse and untied the coat from behind the saddle. The others had kept their coats on, and they pulled up the collars against the sudden raw wind.

The only person not wearing a hat was Josefina. The heavy wool coat she wore was equipped with a hood. Rosa reached where the child sat beside her, and pulled the hood over her head.

As Wolf shouldered into his coat, Pedro Llamas said, "The wind is carrying the cold down from the snow on the high peaks. From the feel of it, I would say there is some weather on the way."

Chapter Nine

Pedro Llamas's prediction proved to be accurate. By midafternoon, Wolf Bixler and his five companions were watching ominous black clouds gather over the high, snowcapped peaks. Progress was slow in the rugged mountain country, but the small column of riders moved steadily on.

As the biting wind clawed at his bearded face, Wolf called to the man ahead of him. "Will we get snow at this elevation, Pedro?"

"No," he replied, turning around in his saddle. "The snow will only be on the highest peaks. We will get rain here. We are at about six thousand feet." Studying the dark, swirling clouds for a moment, he said, "I think it is going to be severe. We should try to make it to a cave, where we can get in out of the weather for the night. I know of one right on our route."

"How long till we reach it?"

"Two hours, at least."

"Then I think we are going to get wet," Wolf said. "I don't think those clouds can hold their water that long."

"You are right," agreed the guide. "It is going to break loose very soon."

The rain held off for another hour. At first the sky began to spit, sending irritating little drops into the eyes of the travelers. But within ten minutes, rain was coming hard, the wind getting stronger. Moments later, the storm hit in all of its fury, and the rain came down in torrents, driven by a fierce, cold wind.

"We are heading for a cave I know about!" Pedro shouted past Diego Corral and Josefina to the others. "It is at the edge of a canyon! We will be there shortly!"

The trail toward the lip of the canyon was on a steep decline. The horses began to slip and slide in the mud and on the wet rocks. At one point, Diego's mount lost its footing, dropping to one knee, and the sudden movement almost dislodged Diego and Josefina from the saddle.

The frightened child let out a wail and began to cry.

"It is all right, now," Diego told her as the animal regained its footing. "We are fine."

The man's words had no effect. The tragic events of the past few days, the flight for her life, and the fury of the violent storm had taken their toll on Josefina Montoya. The stumbling of the horse had unleashed the child's pent-up emotions, and she wept and wailed at the top of her voice.

Diego pulled rein, allowing Rosa's horse to come alongside him. Leaning from the saddle with rain dripping off the brim of her flat-crowned hat, she tried to console Josefina, but to no avail. The wailing continued.

Diego clutched her tight to his chest. "She will be all right!" he told Rosa above the storm and Josefina's crying. Rosa pulled back in line behind him, but Josefina continued to cry, in spite of Diego's soothing words.

After some ten or fifteen minutes of the child's sobbing, Wolf Bixler's patience wore thin. Children were a source of annoyance to him to begin with, and this high-pitched wailing was cutting at his nerves like a rusty saw.

Pivoting in the saddle, Diego looked back at Wolf with rain dripping from his hat and saw the man scowl. Rosa also turned and looked into his irritated face, knowing his anger was about to spill. She wished he would not do it. Josefina was already frightened enough.

Then it came, exploding from Wolf's wide mouth. *"Corral! Shut that kid up!"*

Diego Corral, a man of congenial manner and pleas-

ant personality, did not understand the gritty ways or
flinty temperament of a man like Wolf Bixler. He himself seldom felt anger. But this was too much, even for
an easygoing man.

A burning anger filled Diego's chest. Lifting his voice,
he shouted, "Have you no understanding, Bixler? Josefina
is only a *child*! She has never traveled like this before!
It is only natural for her to be frightened! Do you have
no feelings? This little thing has just seen her parents
and grandmother buried, killed by assassins' bullets!
She *knows* that she and her aunt and uncle are fleeing
for their lives! Where is your heart, Wolf Bixler?"

The fiery, undimmed anger in Diego's eyes burned
Wolf's face through the driving rain. Wolf glared back
for a moment and then swung his head down.

Rosa gave Diego a warm smile.

In less than a minute, Josefina's wailing subsided.
She sobbed quietly for a few minutes, but that couldn't
be heard by anyone but Diego because of the pounding
rain. He continued speaking soft words of comfort in
her ears until she stopped crying altogether.

The rain was still driving hard when Pedro led the
weary travelers to the mouth of a large cave carved into
a steep, rocky slope. They could barely see their sur-
roundings in the near darkness.

Rosa took Josefina into the protection of the cave
while the men and Armand unsaddled the horses. Pedro carried his saddle inside, dropped it on dry ground,
and said to Rosa, "The last time I was here, there was
wood piled in this cave." Fishing inside his dripping
coat to a shirt pocket, he produced a dry match and
struck it against the wall. Cupping the flame with his
other hand, he moved deeper into the black cavity. A
sound of happy surprise came from his mouth, and he
returned, bearing an armload of wood.

Five minutes later the whole complexion of things
had changed. While the wind howled and the rain
roared outside, Pedro's fire brought cheer to the weary
travelers and welcome warmth to their chilled bones.
Rosa cooked a meal, and spirits were lifted as the hot
food was shared.

Diego Corral, who had the heart of a clown, showed everyone how many funny-looking faces he could make. Their burdensome journey was soon temporarily forgotten, and light-hearted laughter filled the cave. Josefina especially enjoyed the antics of the wiry little rubber-faced man, and the fears she had experienced earlier in the day were dispelled.

The only person who did not laugh was Wolf Bixler, though Diego did hold his attention.

When the show was over, conversation around the fire was kept to light subjects. No one mentioned the long journey that lay ahead or the dangers that shadowed their path.

The rain was still pounding the rocky slope outside the cave when Josefina began to rub her tired eyes. Rosa saw it and said, "All right, señorita, it is time for you to go to bed. You give everybody a love while I fix your bedroll."

The little Mexican girl made the rounds hugging necks. Armand came first, then "Uncle" Diego. From Diego, she went to Pedro. As Josefina pulled away from the stout-bodied guide, her black eyes went to the bearded man sitting cross-legged, Indian style, facing the fire. Shadows flickered on his formidable face.

Everyone could see that Josefina was hesitant to go to Wolf because of the way he had spoken of her earlier in the day. Wolf kept his gaze on the fire, as if feeling the weight of those big black eyes and hoping she would just go on to bed.

But Josefina put the big crusty man off balance again. She moved in and wrapped her arms around his neck, squeezing him tight. He made no move to embrace her. The child's affection embarrassed him, but he did not know how to escape her.

After Josefina was tucked into bed, Rosa made coffee and set the pot over the fire. The wind and rain continued, not easing in the smallest degree.

Armand, full of admiration for Wolf, looked across the fire to him and said, "Señor, Papa told me that you were raised by Comanche Indians."

Wolf's dark eyes fixed on the finely chiseled face of the

youth. He was beginning to like Armand. There was something about him. . . . Wolf could not put his finger on it, but they seemed to have in common some kindred spirit.

"Yes." The somber man nodded.

"What happened to your real parents?" enquired Armand.

"I don't know," Wolf replied. "The Comanches found me wandering on the plains of west Texas all alone. I was no more than five years old."

"You were raised in Texas?"

"Yes."

"Does that make you a Texan?"

"I don't know, son," the big man said. "I never thought about whether I was a Texan or not. Why?"

"My tutor taught me that Texans are bad," responded the curly-headed youth. "He told us about how they stole the big land from Mexico. They are dirty *diablos*! But our great General Antonio López de Santa Anna took his brave soldiers to San Antonio de Behar and made them sorry. He killed a whole lot of those dirty *diablos* at the Alamo in March of eighteen thirty-six."

"Boy knows his history," Wolf said to Pedro Llamas.

Pedro closed his eyes and opened them in silent assent.

"Guess I'm not a Texan," Wolf said, setting his eyes on Armand again. "Texans are white men. I'm white on the outside, but I'm Indian on the inside. What's inside makes you what you really are. Nope, I ain't no Texan."

"Good!" exclaimed the youth. "Tell me what it is like to be an Indian."

Rosa was amazed to see Wolf Bixler being more congenial to her brother than he had been to anyone in the group. She knew, however, that if given enough time and ample opportunity, Josefina would win him over.

Wolf sat by the fire and talked to the dark-skinned youth until they finally noticed that everyone else had climbed in their bedrolls and gone to sleep. Wolf threw more wood on the fire, and the two of them bedded down for the night.

Dawn came with a hush over the mountains. The travelers awoke, realizing that both the rain and the wind had stopped. One by one, they crawled from their bedrolls and walked to the mouth of the cave, where their eyes beheld the vast canyon that yawned before them. The rim of the chasm was only fifty feet away. From somewhere in its rocky depths a river sent a loud roar through the hollow stillness, its watery rumble echoing off unseen granite walls.

Diego Corral breathed in the fresh scent of wet pine and commented that judging from the sound of the river in the canyon, the heavy rain must have turned it into a roaring monster.

Calmly, Pedro Llamas informed the group that they must descend into the canyon and cross it, roaring monster or not. The river lay directly across their path.

With stomachs full of Rosa's cooking, the group was mounting up to pull out. Pedro was the last to leave the cave. Stepping into the stirrup, he said to Wolf, who was already mounted, "I wish we could have replaced the wood we used. But there is enough left in the cave to supply someone for a full night."

As the group wound down the steep trail into the canyon, the sun put in an appearance for a short while, but then it disappeared behind a heavy cloud cover. Wolf eyed the gray canopy above the towering trees and wondered if more rain was on the way.

After nearly two hours, the river with its white turbulence came into view some three hundred feet below. The angry waters seemed eager to make their way from the ragged mountains to the quiet calm of the sea.

Another half hour brought them to the canyon floor and the bank of the winding river. Josefina stared at the roiling, foamy water, eyes wide.

"We'll have to ride along the bank and find the best

place to cross!" Llamas shouted to the others above the deafening roar.

Armand noticed a dead animal about the size of a small deer floating in the rushing river, but he decided not to point it out. Everyone was nervous enough about the prospect of entering the turbulent waters.

Wolf spoke up loudly "All of you wait here. I'm going to ride downstream for a ways. If I don't see a likely spot, I'll come back, and we'll take a look upstream."

The others huddled in their coats against the chill as Wolf Bixler guided his horse along the rocky bank. At one spot some sixty yards downstream, he came upon a narrow place where the rushing water had torn away part of the bank. There were heavy bushes to his left, and the river was on his right. He thought about turning back, but then saw a bend in the river another fifty yards ahead. It looked as if the river bed might widen from that spot.

Under the group's watchful gaze, he inched the big sorrel past the narrow place. Bushes clawed at his left leg, but man and horse made it through.

Within half a minute, Wolf disappeared around the bend. He was gone for about three minutes and then came around the bend and halted the sorrel. Motioning with his arm, he signaled for the others to come ahead. He had found a likely spot to cross. Pointing at the narrow place where part of the bank had washed away, he signaled a warning for them to be careful.

As Pedro nudged his horse forward, Wolf wheeled his mount and again disappeared around the bend. Behind Pedro came Rosa. The bushes scratched at them as they squeezed by the narrow spot, but both of them made it.

Next in line was Diego Corral, with the child riding in front of him. As they approached the narrow place, the horse became skittish, and Diego, speaking above the sound of the river, attempted to calm the animal. Josefina felt the horse's fear and clung hard to the saddle horn, her huge eyes fixed on the turbulent, foamy water.

Touching spurs gently to the animal's sides, Diego said, "Come on, boy. You can make it. The others did."

The horse obeyed, crowding the bushes tightly, but when its right forefoot touched the bank near the broken edge, more ground broke loose, and the animal's leg suddenly dropped. Josefina screamed as horse and riders plunged into the raging river.

Rosa and Pedro saw the fall from where they sat. Rosa froze, her throat constricted as she saw Diego and Josefina disappear into the swirling rapids.

From behind, Armand leaped from his horse, ran beyond the narrow spot, and darted past Pedro, who had just left his saddle. The boy was peeling off his coat, getting ready to dive in. Rosa screamed at him, "No, Armand! You will drown!"

Dropping his gun belt, throwing down hat and coat, Pedro said, "You stay ashore, Armand! Take the lariat from my saddle and run downriver as fast as you can! Get ahead of us, and be ready to throw it!"

Not waiting for a reply, Pedro ran down the bank himself, his eyes searching the violent waters. Suddenly he saw Diego and Josefina surface in the middle of the river, adjacent to where he stood. Josefina was thrashing wildly, just out of Diego's reach. Swirling away from him, she vanished.

Pedro ran farther along the bank, beyond the child and Diego, and dived in. Armand charged down the riverbank behind, carrying the rope, with Rosa on his heels.

Downstream, Wolf Bixler, figuring the others should have come around the bend by then, turned back to investigate. When he saw Rosa and Armand climbing down the bank, he shot his gaze to the waters. There he saw three bobbing heads. Diego and Pedro were neck and neck, trying to get to Josefina, who was now thirty feet ahead of them, frantic, her small arms flailing.

Wolf tore off hat, gun belt, bandoliers, and boots, his eye trained on the little girl who was speedily being swept toward him. Gauging her speed and line of travel, he ran to the raging river's edge and hurled himself in.

Battling the powerful current, he intercepted Josefina

and took her in his grasp. She clung to him with a death grip. Steadily, Wolf fought his way toward the bank, and minutes later, he was lifting himself and the terrified child out of the roiling foam onto the bank.

When Armand saw that Wolf was going to make it all right, he threw the rope to the two men and pulled them ashore.

Rosa met Wolf and took Josefina from him, patting the child solidly on the back. Josefina was coughing, but she was able to breathe all right.

Wolf went to Diego Corral to ask how the accident had happened, and Diego gave a quick explanation. Satisfied there had been no carelessness on Corral's part, Wolf asked Pedro if he knew of any nearby caves. The closest one, Pedro told him, was where they had spent the night.

It was not until Wolf pointed to the sky that Pedro realized the rain was again falling.

Diego's horse had found solid ground somewhere and climbed out of the river, apparently uninjured. He was waiting with Rosa and Pedro's horses on the bank.

Rosa wrapped Josefina in her serape. The child was quivering, and her teeth were chattering.

Looking at the child, Wolf announced, "We'll try to cross the river tomorrow, when it's not so rough. Right now let's climb back to the cave and build a fire, so we can all dry out."

The way it was raining, even Armand and Rosa, who had not gone in the river, would be soaked by the time they got to the cave.

Armand spotted a natural path leading into the thicket that bypassed the dangerous narrow spot but would lead them back to his mount and the packhorse. Josefina rode with Rosa, wrapped in the serape, as the exhausted group climbed out of the canyon.

It was still raining lightly when they reached the cave and built a fire. While everybody huddled close to the fire's warmth, Rosa said to Pedro, "I want to thank you for trying to save my niece. It was a brave thing for you to do."

Pedro smiled. "Gracias, señorita," he said. "I am

only sorry I did not reach her before Wolf had to get wet."

Rosa patted his arm and then looked across the fire at the big man. "I am in your debt, Señor Wolf," she said sincerely. "Please know that what you did is deeply appreciated. Had it not been for you, Josefina would have drowned."

"You don't owe me anything, girl," replied Wolf in his brusque way. "No man could just stand by and watch someone drown."

Rosa wondered why the man found it necessary to hide in his tough shell. Why could he not show a little warmth and human sympathy?

Without provocation from anyone, Josefina stood up from where she sat next to Rosa. Dragging the serape that was wrapped around her, she circled the fire and approached Wolf, who sat cross-legged on the dirt floor. Wrapping her small arms around his thick neck, she planted a kiss on his cheek and then hugged him, saying, "Thank you, Uncle Wolf, for saving my life."

Rosa and Armand eyed each other and traded furtive smiles when they saw the flush on Wolf's face. His dark eyes softened for an instant when Josefina called him "Uncle Wolf," but then resumed their usual stern look.

Again, the man did not raise a hand to return the affection. When Josefina released her embrace, he said to her, "I was glad to save your life, but I am not your uncle, little black-eyed girl."

Rosa and Armand again smiled at each other. Little Josefina had just put a crack in Wolf Bixler's tough shell.

Chapter Ten

The sun shone bright through the broken clouds, with the promise of warmth to dull the frosty air's bite.

United States marshal Stuart Jarrell let his gaze stray across the mesquite-covered hills as the stage driver shouted from the box up above, "San Antonio, straight ahead!"

The stagecoach rocked along at an angle that gave Jarrell a clear view of the old town. He could see the San Antonio River snaking southeasterly across the plains, rolling lazily through the town, and wending its way toward the Gulf of Mexico.

Jarrell saw that San Antonio's uneven skyline was composed of houses and commercial structures with rooftops of varied shapes and angles. Standing above them all was the bell tower of the old San Fernando church.

Jarrell was glad to be arriving in San Antonio. Wolf Bixler would be south of the Mexican border by now, and so the marshal had decided to ride a stage from Waco to San Antonio to get some much-needed rest. What he hadn't counted on was that four elderly women would be on the stagecoach with him all the way from Waco. He was the only man. He felt as if he had been an unwanted guest at a hen party.

Presently the coach rolled into town and wheeled up to the Lone Star Stage Company office. Doing the gentlemanly thing, the young marshal alighted from the vehicle first and then helped the ladies down. Upon asking the driver, he learned that the livery stable was two blocks up the street.

As he turned and walked in that direction, he could hear the sound of a guitar coming from somewhere, accompanying a male voice singing a song in Spanish.

The population of the town seemed mostly Mexican. Wide-brimmed sombreros and bright-colored serapes were everywhere. There were crude-wheeled oxcarts and horsedrawn wagons moving along the dusty street.

In a shadowed doorway Jarrell saw a young couple clinched in an embrace. He thought of Peggy Garner. Why did she have to be so stubborn? Couldn't she understand that when a man finds his path in life he has to follow it? If she thought he was going to come crawling back, she had another think coming.

Jarrell passed the sheriff's office, noting by the sign that the sheriff of Bexar County was Ted Traxler. He had heard that name before, but had never met the man.

Suddenly his attention was drawn up ahead, where people were scurrying away from the front of the Yellow Rose Saloon. A lone man, with his back to Jarrell, was facing four dirty, rough-looking men, who stood shoulder to shoulder. His hand hovered over the low-slung holster on his hip.

Pushing his way among the people who milled about on the wooden sidewalk, the young federal marshal inconspicuously moved closer. Hanging back in the shade of a canopy, he listened as one of the unkempt men said, "If you're gonna arrest Hardy, Sheriff, you'll have to go through the rest of us."

Jarrell's hunch was right. The lone man facing the four hardcases was Ted Traxler.

"Your pal Hardy is the one who threw the bottle and broke the mirror behind the bar, Dick," Traxler said calmly. "You heard him yourself. I told him to fork over the fifty dollars to replace the mirror, or it's sixty days in jail. He says it's neither. Well, he's wrong. It's one or the other."

Stuart Jarrell observed the bartender, wearing a white

apron, standing just outside the swinging saloon doors. A towel was draped over his shoulder as he looked on with apprehension.

"Not as long as there's breath in our bodies, Traxler," breathed the one called Dick. "So you can go for that gun and try your luck, or you can turn and walk away. Choice is yours."

"L-look, Ted," the bartender nervously spoke up, "you c-can't take on four men all by yourself. J-just let it go. It isn't w-worth it."

"No, Duff," the sheriff said to the bartender without taking his eyes off his challengers. "There is principle here. Nobody can come into this town and tear up people's property and just walk away. If I tolerate that, the next thing they'll do is shoot anybody they don't like and take over the town. Hardy's going to pay you for the mirror or go to jail."

Jarrell ran his gaze over the few people who had not scattered. Apparently no one was going to help the sheriff.

The man called Dick thrust out his unshaven jaw and said, "It's like he told you, Sheriff. Hardy ain't doin' neither."

The sheriff stood poised, knowing he was in trouble.

"Better think it over, Traxler," rasped Dick. "You're all alone."

"No, he's not!" came a sharp, loud voice.

Stuart Jarrell's words hit Dick like the blade of an ax. His jaw snapped shut.

Ted Traxler didn't dare take his eyes from the four men, but in the periphery of his vision he saw a tall, rawboned figure move next to him.

"This ain't none of your affair, Marshal," said Dick, noting the badge on Jarrell's coat.

"I'm making it my affair," Jarrell retorted.

"We've still got twice as many men as you," warned Hardy.

"Best thing for you boys to do," Jarrell advised, "is to pay for the broken mirror and get on your ponies." Dick opened his mouth to speak, but the marshal beat him to it. "You can make this street a graveyard if you want to, mister," he said with clipped words, "but I'd think you'd rather cough up the money."

"It'll be your graveyard, Marshal!" Dick snarled. With that, he went for his gun.

Instantly Jarrell drew, and his gun spit fire. While Dick was bounding backward from the impact of the slug in his heart, the other three clawed at their weapons.

Traxler shot one of the men, and Jarrell drilled another. In the fracas, Hardy was bumped by the man Traxler had shot, and he dropped his gun. Stuart Jarrell stepped in and clouted him solidly on the head with his gun barrel. Hardy collapsed in a heap.

Gun smoke stung their nostrils as the two lawmen examined Dick and his two bloody cohorts. Those three were dead, and Hardy lay motionless. People began to gather around, shock and curiosity registered on their faces.

Ted Traxler slid his gun into his holster and looked at Jarrell, smiling. Extending his hand, he said, "I see by your badge that you're a federal marshal. But your name isn't on it."

Matching Traxler's grip, the tall man said, "Jarrell, Sheriff. Stuart Jarrell."

Still smiling, Traxler sighed. "I don't know where you came from, Jarrell, but I'm sure glad you showed up! There's no way I could have taken all four of them."

"Don't you have a deputy?"

"Yes, but he's sick, so I'm going it alone."

Hardy began to stir.

"Well," said Jarrell, "at least you can put Hardy in jail without any interference now."

"Yeah," agreed Traxler, leaning over to pick up Hardy's gun. Speaking to the men who had gathered around, he said, "One of you go tell Myron he's got three corpses to bury."

One of the men hastened away to find the undertaker.

"Gather up their guns," he commanded the others. Turning back to Jarrell, he asked, "Where'd you come from and where are you bound, Marshal?"

Jarrell answered the question in brief, adding that he had best be on his way.

"Least you can do is let me buy you a drink," said Traxler.

"Have to be another time, Sheriff." Jarrell adjusted the gray Stetson on his head. "I really must hit the trail."

Shaking Jarrell's hand again, Traxler said, "I don't know how to thank you, Marshal."

"No need," grinned the square-jawed man. "You were a fellow lawman in trouble. Just doing my duty." He glanced at the groggy outlaw on the ground and then walked away.

Less than an hour later the United States marshal came out of the general store and tied a bundle behind the saddle of the big dun gelding he had purchased at the livery stable. Swinging into the saddle, he headed out of town.

Jarrell was weaving among the busy traffic, when he looked up at a sign on the corner just ahead. He was about to cross Travis Street. His mind flashed back to his history books. *William Barrett Travis. Died March 6, 1836, while leading the Texan troops defending the Alamo.* He could remember the day of the month because March sixth was his mother's birthday.

Reining in at the corner, he looked up and down Travis Street. There it was, a half block to his left. Stuart Jarrell was a dyed-in-the-wool Texan, but he had never been to San Antonio. As pressed as he was to be on the trail of Wolf Bixler, he could not pass this opportunity.

Touching spurs to the dun's sides, he rode toward the old Franciscan mission known as the Alamo.

He drew near the walled mission and, halting at the front gate, gazed around the rectangular complex. Rising up out of the sun baked, wind swept prairie, the Alamo stood as a monument to the one hundred eighty-two gallant men who fought the forces of General Antonio López de Santa Anna to make Texas a free and sovereign republic.

The mission was an impressive sight. The large rectangular court, covering three acres, was framed by stone walls three feet thick and nine to twelve feet

high. There were several flat-roofed buildings that had
been used as barracks and storage houses when it was a
military fort in 1801.

Peering through the iron-barred gate, Jarrell noted
that the doors and windows of all but one building had
been boarded up.

His attention was drawn to the eastern edge of the
enclosure, where the two largest buildings in the Alamo
stood. The greatest in size was the two-story convent
that had been the main barracks. It, too, was boarded
up.

Stuart Jarrell thought it a shame that a place of such
historical significance was not kept in good repair. It
should be kept and maintained for future generations to
see and appreciate.

The other large building, about fifty feet from the
convent, was the chapel. It was the only building not
boarded up. Its flat roof was accentuated by a huge
scalloped stone wall at the front edge. Just below that,
on the face of the battle-pocked chapel, were the huge
grooved columns flanking four niches where stone stat-
ues once stood.

Jarrell saw that the big iron gate was not locked. He
had the urge to dismount, pass through it, and see if he
could get inside the chapel. But he fought the urge,
telling himself that he had to be on his way to Mexico.

Wheeling the horse, the marshal rode down the dusty,
rutted street. Before turning the corner, he stopped
and looked back at the Alamo, and for a moment, he
visualized that fateful day. He could see the Mexican
soldiers in their bright uniforms throwing ladders against
the walls. He could hear the shouting of fighting men,
the pop of muskets, and the deep boom of the cannons.
It became so real that he could smell the burnt powder
as he listened to the roar of the battle.

Suddenly, he was back to the present. The Alamo
stood in a ghostly silence, silhouetted against the blue
sky.

Swinging his gaze to the southwest, the youthful
lawman thought of Wolf Bixler. A man of Bixler's cut

and impressive size could not travel unnoticed. Jarrell figured his trail would be relatively simple to follow.

After one more lingering look at the Alamo, Stuart Jarrell clucked to his horse and headed for Mexico.

Wolf Bixler had been right. The river was less turbulent the morning after Josefina Montoya and Diego Corral had fallen in, and they all crossed it without incident.

But after another day had passed, Josefina had developed a runny nose and a sore throat. When the travelers neared a village in late morning, Rosa suggested to Wolf that she be allowed to take the child there to find a doctor, but he had refused, saying it was best that none of them be seen, especially she and the little girl. They could be too easily identified.

The air was cold, and the wind was sweeping down through the valleys and canyons. Josefina rode with Rosa, wrapped in the serape with the hood of her coat pulled over her head. Rosa had decided that if Josefina got worse, she would take her to a doctor in spite of Wolf Bixler's wishes.

As the group moved across a mountain plateau among scattered brush, Rosa took advantage of the more open country to pull her horse alongside Wolf's. She hoped that if she showed more interest in him, he might be friendlier toward her. It had worked for Armand. If Wolf sweetened up some, the journey would be more pleasant.

Rosa was unaware of the smile little Josefina was giving the big bearded man as the two horses drew parallel. Wolf tried to ignore the child, but the smile was infectious. Her innocent friendliness knocked him off balance.

"Josefina likes you, Señor Wolf," Rosa said when she realized what her niece was doing.

Wolf did not comment. He pulled his gaze from the smile and looked forward, scanning the brush country as if looking for any movement.

Rosa spoke up. "You were telling Armand about your

life with the Indians the other night, Señor Wolf. Why are you not living with them still?"

Wolf began to describe the problems that had developed between himself and some of the Comanche braves as he grew into manhood. He told her about the raw treatment he had received from the white men and his subsequent breaking of their laws.

"I can understand why you would have bitterness in your heart," she commented.

For a few moments, all was quiet except for the sound of the horses' hooves on the soft earth, the whine of a light wind, and an occasional sniffle from Josefina.

Then Rosa broached a new subject. "Señor Wolf, has there ever been a woman in your life?"

He cast her a sidelong glance and mumbled, "Only Red Fawn."

"An Indian girl?"

"No. My adopted Comanche mother."

"Oh. But you have never been in love?"

"Never had time to get involved with women," he replied, his voice taking on a defensive crust. "Women expect a man to be softhearted and sentimental. I am neither. Besides, what woman would take a second look at an ugly man like me?"

Rosa wanted to be careful how she responded to Wolf's self-degrading words. He certainly was not a handsome man, but neither did she consider him ugly. Though much of his face was covered with his heavy black beard, several scars were visible. The most noticeable was the white-ridged scar running from the corner of his right eye to his ear, which looked as if a dog had chewed off the top of it.

But apart from the scars, Rosa saw nothing ugly about him. She was about to contradict him when Josefina sniffed and said, "I do not think you are ugly, Uncle Wolf. I think you are handsome."

Rosa saw Wolf's composure rupture for a brief instant at the child's words. Embarrassed by it, he grumbled, "I am not your uncle, little black-eyed girl."

*   *   *

It was late in the afternoon, and five swarthy-skinned Mexicans peered over the edge of their rocky perch above the narrow valley.

Carlos Ortega, the leader of the bandits, was looking through binoculars at the five horses moving below. "Oh, ho!" he said gleefully. "Six riders, and one of them is a delicious señorita!"

"Oh?" exclaimed Goliad Barca, reaching for the binoculars. "Let me see!"

Ortega swatted Goliad's grimy hand away, swearing angrily. "You will see when I say!" he snapped, looking through the binoculars again. "She has a child in her arms, I think. She rides behind a large man. He must be her husband."

"If she has a husband and a child, Carlos, she is a señora," corrected Barca. Chuckling, he said, "Sometimes I think you are not so smart, Carlos!"

Ortega's dark face twisted into a scowl. "One of these days I am going to put a bullet into your big mouth, Goliad!"

"I think you two had better stop arguing," spoke up Lorenzo Mechara. "We must hurry down to meet our prey."

"Ho, ho!" laughed Ortega. "We will not only take their horses, and money, and guns. We will also take the delicious señorita!" Shooting a glance at Barca, he added, "Or señora."

The other three grinned wickedly in anticipation.

The five bandits rode a steep, winding path down the slope amid rocks, boulders, and brush. Reaching level ground, they tied their mounts in a gully and scrambled to a spot where they could see the riders approaching.

Carlos Ortega pointed out a place in the path of the riders where they would pass through a narrow ravine. He and his partners would spring upon them, guns drawn, once they were there and could not scatter or spread out.

"They will be easy pickings," Ortega murmured, a lecherous smirk on his face.

*   *   *

Pedro Llamas, spotting the narrow ravine a hundred yards away, turned from his lead position and told Wolf Bixler to keep on a straight line through it. He wanted to drop back and talk to Armand for a while.

Pedro and the boy were talking as the procession moved single file into the narrow stretch. They were between two brush-covered dirt banks only six feet apart.

Wolf Bixler's sixth sense warned of trouble only seconds before the five bandits jumped in front of him. He had just pulled rein, responding to instinct. Five threatening muzzles pointed at him in front of ten wicked-looking eyes. Everyone in the procession pulled to a halt, waiting for him to decide what to do.

Grinning under floppy sombreros, the bandits blocked the path, standing in a semicircle where the ravine widened out. With a heinous grin, the leader said to him, *"Buenas tardes, señor.* We will now relieve you of your horses, your guns, and your money. We will also take the beautiful señorita. If you give us trouble, we will kill you and take what we want anyway."

Wolf knew he would have to act fast. There was only one thing he could do.

Ortega was telling them all to raise their hands, when the big man gouged his horse violently with his heels. The startled animal lunged, plowing through the *banditos* like a charging freight train. Ortega took the brunt of the charge. The horse hit him in the face with its muzzle, knocking him down and stepping on his stomach.

Mechara and Barca were bumped hard and sent rolling.

As he sent the sorrel into the bandits, Wolf was drawing one of the Colts. The Mexicans on the ends of the semicircle had to leap aside to keep from being hit, throwing them off balance. This gave Wolf time to pivot the horse and draw the other revolver.

Both guns spit fire. The bandits on the ends were cut down as they were bringing their guns to bear.

Wolf's weapons barked again, as Mechara and Barca were gaining their feet. Both were struck dead center in their chests and died before they hit the ground.

Carlos Ortega rose to one knee, picking his revolver up with his right hand and holding his bulging, injured stomach with the left. His head was spinning. The big man on the sorrel was a fuzzy blur, but Ortega would shoot at him anyway.

He never got a chance.

Wolf Bixler put two .45 slugs in his chest, killing him instantly.

While Wolf's guns roared, little Josefina clung hard to Rosa but did not cry out. Rosa pulled her horse on through the draw, allowing the men behind her to follow. As the light wind carried the gun smoke away, Armand dismounted at the same time Wolf did. Dashing to him while pulling off his hat, the boy excitedly exclaimed, "That was great shooting, Wolf! I never saw anything like that in my whole life!" His black curly hair dropped in an unruly manner on his forehead, and beneath it admiration beamed out of his chocolate-brown eyes.

Rosa knew that Wolf had saved her from a horrible fate, but she was disturbed that he was becoming her brother's idol. Armand was impressed by Wolf Bixler's skill with weapons, his iron nerve, and his hard approach to life. Just the day before, Rosa had noticed that Armand was trying to imitate Wolf's walk.

Pedro and Diego complimented the bearded man on his adept handling of the bandits.

"Was not that dangerous, though?" asked Diego. "Were you not concerned about being able to get all five of them?"

"No," Wolf answered flatly.

"Not at all?"

"No. It's all in the timing. They gave me the opportunity to get the upper hand. All I had to do was time it right."

Rubbing his chin in amazement, Armand said, "Timing really is important, right, Wolf?"

"Yeah," he replied, messing up Armand's hair. "Like when you're eatin'. If you don't open your mouth at just the right time when you're bringin' the fork up, you'll get food on your face."

Chapter Eleven

The next morning Josefina's cold was worse. She was coughing now, and Rosa was sure she had a fever.

As the group rode away from the spot where they had camped for the night, Rosa said to Wolf, "We have to get Josefina to a doctor. I must take her into the next village we come near."

Wolf held firm, saying, "If any of us let ourselves be seen where people are concentrated, our chances for makin' it to San Antonio grow slimmer. The Federales are only lookin' for me, but the assassins, if they get the information, will be lookin' for all of us. That includes you and the little black-eyed girl. We've got to stay away from the villages except to get supplies . . . and then we must do it as carefully as possible, by sendin' in one of us men. You catch too many male eyes, girl, and the child is too noticeable. I just can't let you take her into a village."

Rosa's indignation flared. "Josefina will get *worse* unless she is treated!" she said hotly. "She could get pneumonia and die! You are good at killing men, Señor Wolf. Do you also kill children?"

Her words cut into him like the snarling tip of a bullwhip. He knew Rosa was right; the child was getting sicker. The risk would have to be taken. They would stop at the next village they came to, he promised her, and he and the others would wait outside in the brush while Rosa took Josefina into the village to see if there was a doctor.

Rosa called to Pedro Llamas, who was in the lead, and asked if he knew of a village up ahead. But he had not been in this exact area before and knew of nothing that would not take them well out of their way. Little Josefina would have to hold on till they came to a village along the chosen route.

As the day passed slowly, the group rode in stolid silence. Josefina's cough was going deeper into her lungs. Rosa held her close, noticing growing concern for the little girl among the men.

With no sign of a settlement nearby, they made camp at sundown. They were still high in the Sierra Madres, and the air turned bitter cold as darkness fell. Diego held Josefina, keeping her warm by the fire, while Rosa cooked the meal.

Later, as the men were preparing to bed down, Rosa sat by the fire, the sick child cradled in her arms. Diego stepped close and said, "Rosa, if you want Josefina to be kept by the fire all night, I will take her so you can sleep without her coughing keeping you awake."

"No, you go ahead, Diego," she said. "I will be fine."

Abruptly, a deep voice said, "We'll trade off, girl. Then nobody will miss a night's sleep."

Rosa looked up to see Wolf Bixler towering over her, outlined against the star-studded sky. She was stunned—he was actually offering to hold Josefina and sit by the fire to keep her warm.

It was obvious to everyone that Wolf had developed a liking for Armand, but his lack of warmth toward Josefina had made them wonder if he would ever let down his guard with her. Yet Rosa had observed that the amiable attitude of Josefina toward Wolf, and the affection she had shown him, were subtly chipping away at his hard shell. This offer proved her right.

Rosa talked with the others, and each agreed to take a turn with Josefina, Wolf being the first. Rosa would get some sleep and then take a two-hour shift, and Pedro, Diego, and Armand would follow in that order.

If each of the men took a turn, it would be dawn by then, and they could get an early start.

Josefina was asleep when Rosa placed her in Wolf's arms. Nestled against his massive chest, the child appeared to have diminished in size. He held her as if she were made of glass.

Trying not to awaken her, he eased down by the fire. Rosa smiled and walked to the edge of the campsite to pick up her bedroll. For a moment, her gaze swept down across the dark valley below. She looked into the distance for a few minutes and then climbed in the bedroll.

Once everyone was bedded down, Wolf began to relax. He looked down at the sick child in his arms. She had not been the nuisance that he had expected, in truth. For all she had been through recently, Josefina had been quite a trooper.

She does like me, he thought. *Always smilin' at me. Sure is a pretty little thing. Calls me Uncle Wolf. That's kinda sweet. She sure—*

Wolf checked himself. What was he doing, allowing sentimental feelings to take root within him? He quickly turned his thoughts to the long weeks of travel that lay ahead. What kind of trouble would they face next?

He spent the rest of the two-hour shift thinking of the problems that could occur and how to avoid them. Then he awakened Rosa.

Armand Tejada was the first in the camp to stir from sleep at dawn. He rubbed his eyes and sat up, looking at the slumbering forms on the ground. Something was wrong.

It took a few seconds, and then it registered. Diego had not awakened him for his turn with Josefina . . . and there was no one by the fire. In fact, there was no fire. It had gone out. Leaping to his feet, Armand eyed the sleepers. Rosa and Josefina were gone!

In a panic, he quickly rousted the men from their blankets. They searched about in chaos until Pedro pointed out a village nestled among the trees in the valley below. He had not noticed it when they set up camp last night. Diego reported that Rosa's horse was not with the others.

"That's what she's done," said Wolf. "She must've seen lights down there before she crawled in the sack last night. Probably took off as soon as she knew I was asleep. Must've figured I would have made her wait till mornin'."

The men agreed that this could not be left to conjecture. Someone would have to go into the village and make sure Rosa and Josefina were there.

Impetuous under the strain of the moment, big Wolf said, "I'll go. They're my responsibility."

Diego touched his arm. "It is best that one of us *mejicanos* goes, Señor Wolf. Remember the Federales. People would notice you like a white wart on a gorilla's nose."

"I will go," spoke up Pedro.

The others agreed, and the squat-bodied guide prepared for the trip. He was thinking that he would secretly make it a twofold mission. While checking on Rosa and Josefina, he would also wet his whistle at the cantina. He had neglected to bring any whiskey along, and he really needed a good stiff shot.

Dr. Enquito Estrada was awakened by his wife, Maria, telling him that someone was knocking at the front door of the house.

Sleepily, he fumbled for a match and flared a lantern. The knocking was repeated as he headed through the parlor for the door. Pulling it open, he was surprised to see a beautiful young woman holding a bundled-up child in her arms.

"You are Dr. Estrada?" she asked.

"Sí."

"This is my little niece, Josefina. She is very sick."

Stepping back, Estrada said, "Please come in. I will take you to the clinic."

The physician led Rosa through a narrow corridor, into a room that smelled of medicines and antiseptics.

As he examined Josefina, he asked Rosa about the child and where they were from. Rosa told him that they were from Mexico City and were traveling with some other people who were on their way north. Josefina had fallen in a river, been overexposed to the cold, and fallen ill.

Estrada told Rosa that the child was on the verge of pneumonia. She had to be kept warm and dry for several days so that the congestion in her lungs could break up as soon as possible.

"I will prepare her a hot toddy," he said. "It may take two or three, but we must attack the congestion to get that fever down. She must also have a mustard pack on her chest."

Rosa's concern was how to keep Josefina warm and dry while camped outside. She could very well die if she was not cared for properly. The best thing would be for her to stay right here at the clinic with the doctor.

Rosa wondered if she should confide in Estrada. If she told him the situation, he might insist that Josefina be kept under his care. Yet she was afraid to reveal to the doctor her real identity. If his loyalty lay with Porfirio Díaz, he would report it to the wrong people, and she and Josefina would fall into the hands of Díaz's hired killers.

While the dark-eyed woman was pondering her plight, the doctor's plump wife entered the clinic in her robe. "Ah, we have a sick little muchacha," she said, smiling at Josefina.

The little girl, eyes dulled by fever, tried to return the smile, but she could not do it. She coughed with a tight sound in her lungs and lay still.

"This is my wife, Maria," Estrada said softly. "Maria, this is little Josefina and her aunt— You did not tell me your name, señorita."

"My name is Rosa," she replied, looking at Maria.

"They are from Mexico City," the doctor told his wife.

"Mexico City?" echoed the woman. "Rosa, we heard yesterday the bad news that the wicked Díaz sent assassins to kill our beloved El Presidente Tejada. They say he is wounded and some of his family were killed. Do you have any more information on this?"

Rosa's fears instantly vanished.

"Sí," she said, sighing with relief. "My mother and sister and brother-in-law were killed. My father is fleeing, trying to escape the assassins."

Both the Estradas stood wide-eyed, with mouths agape. At last the physician found his voice and said, "*You* are El Presidente's daughter?"

"Sí. I am Rosa Lolita Francisca de Tejada. And the muchacha is Josefina Dolores Consuela Montoya, my murdered sister's daughter."

Maria's hands went to her face as she mumbled something and then crossed herself.

"Then you are also fleeing for your life, no?" the doctor inquired.

Rosa nodded. She told the Estradas the whole story while Maria prepared a hot toddy of whiskey, honey, and lemon juice. Giving Josefina sips of the mixture, the doctor said, "Señorita Tejada, we are most honored to have you and little Josefina in our clinic. Please tell us what we can do to help you."

Rosa asked for shelter for her brother and other traveling companions while Josefina was recuperating. She did not want to endanger the doctor and his wife, but she had nowhere else to turn. They assured her that they loved El Presidente Tejada. The danger meant nothing to them. The travelers were all welcome to stay in their home, where there would be plenty of room for everyone. But they warned that the travelers should come under cover of darkness so as not to be seen.

Estrada put a mustard pack on Josefina and carried her to a bedroom with two beds. He told Rosa to use the other bed and get some sleep. She could ride back to the camp in the morning while he and his wife took care of Josefina.

Rosa was surprised that she had been able to sleep at all when she awoke the next morning. After checking on her slumbering niece, she ate a hearty breakfast with the Estradas and then mounted up and rode out of the village. The sun had been up an hour, and pulling down the brim of her hat, she trotted the horse until she was a good distance from the village, then urged it into a gallop.

Thundering across the valley with the wind in her face, she breathed a prayer of thanks. Little Josefina was in the hands of a good doctor, and the group had a safe place to stay while she was recovering.

Wolf Bixler was giving Diego Corral and Armand Tejada a demonstration of his knife-throwing skills when Rosa came riding through the trees into the camp. She wondered if Wolf would be angry. It was hard to tell, since he wore a scowl all the time. The three men gathered around her as she dismounted.

"Where is Josefina?" queried Armand.

"She is with Dr. Enquito Estrada down in the village of San Rosario," Rosa announced. "He says Josefina is very near having pneumonia. He is taking care of her, but it will be several days before she is well."

Wolf Bixler swore. He was in a hurry to get to San Antonio so he could supply Chief Iron Face with the gold. This delay would cost Comanche lives. Every day without the weapons the gold would buy, Comanches were being slaughtered by the white soldiers.

Diego Corral was irritated at Wolf's burst of profanity in Rosa's presence. "Señor Wolf," he said, looking up at the man towering over him, "I am just a weasel compared to you, but you will apologize to the lady for your crude language, or I will be forced to punch you in the mouth!"

Wolf looked down at the skinny little man, whose jaws were set with determination. Wolf knew he could destroy him with one blow, but he admired a man with spunk. He realized that Diego was right, though he had given the matter no thought before. A lady like Rosa deserved respect and gentlemanly consideration. Turning to her, he muttered, "Diego is right. I apologize."

"Your apology is accepted." Rosa smiled. "I am sorry for this delay, but it cannot be helped." Looking around, she said, "Where is Pedro?"

Wolf gave her an odd look. "Didn't he find you?"

"No. I have not seen him."

Wolf started to swear again, but bit his tongue, glancing sheepishly at Rosa. This confirmed some thoughts he had had about Pedro. The man had eyes that bore the look of one who consumed his share of alcohol. He was probably holed up in a cantina. Suppressing the anger he felt toward Pedro for not returning immediately to the camp, Wolf again turned to Rosa.

"Now let me explain the situation," she said, meeting his gaze.

He listened with the others as she told them of Dr. Estrada's generous offer to house them until Josefina improved. Sighing, he resigned himself to the fact they would go no farther until the little girl could travel.

"We ride in after dark," he said.

Pedro Llamas had still not returned by nightfall. Wolf was seething with anger toward him as the rest of them rode into the village, stashed the horses in the doctor's barn, and took up residence in his house. Wolf and Armand took a room together. Diego would share one with Pedro, whenever they found him.

Estrada told Wolf that Pedro Llamas had shown up on his doorstep that morning looking for Rosa, shortly after she had left for the camp. The doctor added that he had smelled liquor on the man's breath.

"How many cantinas in San Rosario?" Wolf asked.

"Just one," Estrada replied. "It is in the center of the village. Anyone looking for it cannot miss it."

"I've got to go after him," Wolf said with disgust. "If he's drunk, there's no tellin' what might come out of his mouth. He might spill the beans to the wrong person and bring Díaz's assassins right to us."

"It is best that you do not go to the cantina," Diego objected. "You stand out like a—"

"I know," Wolf cut in. "Like a white wart on a gorilla's nose."

Diego chuckled. "I will go after Pedro. I will just be another *mejicano* among *mejicanos*."

"Then it is even better that I go after Pedro," Armand spoke up. "I would be just another *mejicano* kid to these people. Nobody pays any attention to kids."

Armand's reasoning won out, and he left for the cantina after first looking in on his niece. Josefina's fever had broken. Now she could begin to recover.

The curly-haired youth walked along San Rosario's dark main street, following the muffled sound of music and laughter. The night air was cold, urging Armand to walk faster. Reaching the front door of the cantina, he pushed it open and entered a large, smoke-filled room.

A Mexican girl was dancing in the middle of the floor to the music of three guitars. In each hand she held snapping castanets, and as she whirled about, heels clicking on the floor, her brightly colored skirt flared high. The whooping, cheering patrons were clapping to the beat of the music.

Armand threaded his way through the crowd. He had been right—no one paid him any mind. He spotted Pedro Llamas at a table near the edge of the dance floor, playing a card game with three dirty-looking men. One of them was large and beefy and had a mean look in his eyes.

Approaching the table, the boy touched the stout guide's shoulder. "Pedro," he said softly, "it is time to go."

Pedro Llamas lifted his bloodshot eyes and focused them on Armand's features. "Oh, hello, Armand," he slurred, head bobbing. "What'd you say?"

"I said it is time to go, Pedro."

The three Mexicans eyed the boy with scorn, and the big one said in a threatening voice, "You go back to where you came from, kid. Pedro is not going anywhere yet."

The guide laid his cards down and said, "No, Luis. He is right. It is time for me to go."

Luis's dark face went black.

Pedro stood, gathering his winnings and stuffing them in his pockets.

Luis's big fist came down on the table. "No!" he

boomed. "You sit down! I want a chance to win back my money!"

Many faces turned toward the interruption for a moment, but then their attention went back to the dancer, who was still swirling about.

Pedro's face went white, and slowly he sat down.

Armand knew that liquor loosened a man's tongue. If Pedro stayed, he would drink more, and sooner or later he would give away his purpose for being in San Rosario—if he had not already done so.

Taking hold of the man's arm, Armand said, "Come, Pedro. You must go *now*."

Luis's face flamed with anger. Standing, he lashed out and backhanded Armand, the blow sending the boy reeling across the floor. He collided with the dancing girl, and they both went down in a heap.

The music stopped suddenly, as did the clamor. Pensive eyes throughout the room turned to Luis. His hulking body was a threatening pillar of animosity, just hunting an excuse to erupt in violence. Silence fell like a shroud over the cantina.

The liquor causing him to show more courage than was sensible at this moment, Pedro Llamas rose again and spoke to the big man, saying, "Now, Luis, you should not be so rough with the muchacho. He means well."

Luis fixed his dark, ominous eyes on Pedro.

"I am not leaving," Pedro promised. "Please. You will have the opportunity to win back your money."

While Pedro was reasoning with the scowling Mexican, Armand picked himself up, shaking his head to clear it. He took the dancer's hand and helped her to her feet, speaking a word of apology.

When he wiped the back of a hand across his mouth and saw blood, heat seemed to flow up over his face, starting at his collar. His bead-bright eyes grew flecked with anger as a wild impulse raged in him.

The furious boy picked up an unopened whiskey bottle from a nearby table. He moved across the floor, holding it by the neck. Luis's back was to him, so the big man did not hear him coming. No one called out a warning.

Armand swung the bottle with all his strength, smashing it against the man's head. Whiskey and broken glass flew in every direction. Luis, apparently unaffected by the blow, wheeled around slowly, a devil's temper stirring in his fierce eyes.

Armand started to retreat but was too slow, for Luis then sank the fingers of his left hand into the boy's coat. With his right hand, he slapped and backhanded him savagely until Armand's knees buckled. The boy sagged to the floor, stunned, his mouth and nose bleeding.

Quickly, Pedro rammed his hands in his pockets, dumping the money on the table. "Here, Luis," he said, lips trembling, "take your money. I do not want it!"

Sobered by the incident, Pedro helped Armand to his feet. "Come on, boy," he said. "Let us get out of here."

While Pedro and Armand moved toward the door, Luis laughed heartily. Turning to his two friends, he said, "All right, amigos, it is time for another game!"

Chapter Twelve

"**W**e shouldn't have let Armand go," said Wolf Bixler, pacing the parlor floor like a caged beast. "He should have been back by now."

"I will go look for him," volunteered Diego Corral.

Rosa Tejada was sitting on a sofa next to Maria Estrada, worry written on her face. Rising, she went to Diego and said, "It would relieve my mind. He might be having trouble getting Pedro to leave the cantina."

Diego picked up his hat and started toward the door, but at that moment, the sound of shuffling feet came from the porch. Diego pulled open the door, and a bloodied Armand Tejada came through, assisted by Pedro Llamas.

Rosa gasped at the sight of her brother and rushed to him. Dr. Estrada, taking a quick look at the boy, said, "Take him into the clinic."

Wolf Bixler moved in and gathered Armand up in his arms, cradling him like a baby. He looked at Pedro with scorn and said, "Whatever you're going to tell me won't stand as an excuse. This is your fault."

The big man wheeled and carried Armand, following Dr. Estrada into the clinic, and the others came behind them. As Wolf laid the bloody-faced youth on the examining table, he asked, "Who did this, boy?"

Rosa bent over her brother, pushing the hair from his forehead.

"Why not let your friend Pedro tell you about it?" suggested the physician. "Let me work on the boy."

Wolf whirled and looked accusingly at Pedro, florid color blotting his cheeks.

The guide nervously wiped a hand over his sweat-beaded brow. "I . . . I will take the blame," he said, not meeting Wolf's black eyes. "I should have headed right back to the camp. I . . . I just . . . well, I just needed a couple of drinks."

"It took all day and half the night for a couple of drinks?" blared Wolf.

"Well, I, uh—"

"Just get to what happened to the boy," rasped Wolf.

Pedro told the story, naming Luis Arguello as Armand's assailant. Wolf asked for a detailed description of the man, down to every stitch of his clothing. Memorizing the description as Pedro gave it, Wolf said to the guide, "You go back to the cantina and look inside. That's all. Don't go in. Just see if Arguello is still in there. Wait across the street and watch. I'll be along in a few minutes."

Pedro obeyed, disappearing quickly.

Rosa laid a hand on Wolf's arm as he looked over the doctor's shoulder. "What are you going to do, Señor Wolf?" she asked.

Without taking his eyes from Armand's battered and bruised face, Wolf said, "I'm going after the dirty bully who did this to the boy."

"But people will see you," the young woman argued.

"Not if I can help it," parried the angry man. "Anything broken, Doc?"

"No," replied Estrada. "His mouth is cut inside, and both lips are split. His face will have purple marks for a few weeks, but he will be all right."

Armand looked up at Wolf and tried to speak.

"It's okay, boy," said the big man. "Don't try to talk. I'm going to teach that guy a lesson." His words were fringed with violence. As he passed through the clinic door, ducking his head, he said over his shoulder, "I'll be back later. Doc, you take care of that boy."

In the parlor, Wolf shed the twin bandoliers, but

kept the gun belt on in case he needed more than his
fists before this episode was over. Leaving his hat and
coat behind, he stepped out into the frosty night. He
did not notice the cold. His blood was running hot.

In the clinic, Diego Corral looked at Rosa and said,
"One thing for sure. This little *mejicano* is sure glad
he is not Luis Arguello. Señor Wolf will probably hit
Arguello so hard his ancestors will feel it!"

Pedro was waiting in the deep shadows of a boot shop
across the street from the cantina when he saw Wolf
Bixler's hulking form coming up the street.

"Psst! Señor Wolf!" he called in a hoarse whisper.

Wolf angled toward him and drew up, eyeing him in
the vague light.

"He's still in there," whispered Pedro.

"Good," said Wolf. "You can go back to the house
now."

"He has two compadres with him," Pedro reminded
Wolf. "Perhaps I should stay."

"I'll handle it," snapped the angry man.

"Look, I am sorry," said Pedro. "All this is my fault."

"It sure is," Wolf agreed.

"I will not do anything like that again on the whole
trip," Pedro assured him.

"See that you don't. Now git."

Pedro scurried up the street and was instantly swallowed by the darkness. Wolf turned to look at the
cantina. There were no horses tied to the hitch rail in
front of the place. This meant that everyone inside was
a resident of San Rosario or at least was staying somewhere close. To keep from being seen, he would wait
for Luis Arguello to leave and then settle the matter.

Wolf envisioned the big Mexican slapping Armand to
the floor, and his burning fury warmed him, in spite of
the cold night air.

In the next two hours many patrons left the cantina,
but no one answered the description of Luis Arguello.
The music played on, and the laughter continued. Almost another hour had passed when the music died
out. Within moments, people began filing out, laughing
and talking loudly in Spanish.

Wolf Bixler's back straightened when he caught sight of the man fitting Luis Arguello's description. Enough light was coming from the open door of the cantina to make him certain of the man's identity. He was shorter than Wolf—about three inches, he judged—but he appeared to weigh about the same.

Arguello was laughing boisterously. He put his arm around a buxom Mexican woman, and together they started down the street. Wolf followed along on the opposite side, keeping a few steps behind, staying in the shadows.

In less than five minutes Arguello and the woman approached the door of a small adobe house and went inside. Within a few seconds Wolf saw a yellow flare of light, followed by a bright orange glow in three windows.

He wasted no time, his anger still not abated. He bowled his way up to the door and knocked, hoping Arguello would answer. Inside the house, the woman laughed, and then Wolf heard her ask Luis to see who was at the door. Wolf waited in the shadows, keeping back a step from the door. It swung open, throwing a shaft of soft rectangular light on the ground. Arguello could apparently see Wolf's form. "What is it?" he asked, moving into the doorway.

"Luis Arguello?" Wolf asked in his deep voice.

"Sí." Suddenly Arguello felt a powerful hand seize his shirt. His feet left the floor, and he sailed out into the darkness, landing hard in the street. Swearing, he started to get up, but a mountainous form came down on him, driving a knee savagely into his stomach.

Arguello felt a wave of nausea pass through him. Abruptly angry fingers sank into the man's thick hair and pulled the scalp tight. The attacker's knee was still in his stomach, and he howled in pain, attempting to free himself, but he could not do it. The dark figure that held him was strong as a mad bull.

Arguello felt hot breath on his face as his assailant hissed, "You like to beat up on boys, huh? Well, I am going to give you some of your own medicine."

Again, Arguello tried to move, but Wolf's grip in his

hair held firm. The Mexican sucked air through his teeth from the pain.

"Let's see," Wolf said, sand in his voice. "How is it you beat up on a boy? Oh, yes. Like this."

With his free hand, Wolf violently slapped and back-handed Arguello a dozen times. "That's how it feels, Arguello!" he breathed with vengeance. "How do you like it?"

The Mexican groaned and attempted once more to free himself, but Wolf only gripped the hair harder and buffeted him another dozen times.

Wolf became aware of the woman standing in the doorway calling to Arguello. It was too dark for her to see what was happening.

"Luis and I are just havin' a little talk, woman," Wolf spoke up. "He will be in shortly."

"Okay," she responded and shut the door.

Wolf could still make out Arguello's features vaguely by the light coming from the windows. His mouth and nose were bleeding. To make sure the man's lips were well split, he belted his mouth savagely several more times.

With blood bubbling from his nose, Arguello whined, "Please don't hit me anymore!"

"What's the matter, Luis?" Wolf asked mockingly. "If it is good enough for a fifteen-year-old boy, why isn't it good enough for you?"

Wolf stood him on his feet, let go of his hair, and sent a hissing punch to his jaw. Arguello went down, rolling in the dirt. "That's how we do it with a man, isn't it, Luis?" Wolf asked in a tone of derision.

Clambering to his feet, Arguello spit blood and charged the huge figure in front of him, but Wolf hurled his body across the short distance between them and caught Arguello with a sledgehammer blow on the temple. The Mexican dropped as if someone had yanked his feet out from under him.

"Get up!" Wolf bawled. "I'm not through with you!" There was no mercy in him. This brute of a man had dared to lay a hand on Armand.

Arguello rose to his feet again, shaking his head.

Losing was strange and different for him. He was always the aggressor *and* the winner in his fights. So far he had not landed a punch. This would have to change. Aiming at the hulking shadow, he charged, fists pumping.

Wolf timed a head-on blow perfectly and broke the Mexican's nose. Arguello staggered.

Wolf stepped in and brought up a knee cruelly into Arguello's groin. When the Mexican doubled over in agony, Wolf clipped him with an uppercut, straightening him up, and then slammed a punch wickedly to the hollow of his jaw. Arguello toppled like a cut tree and lay still.

Vengeance satisfied, Wolf Bixler headed for the Estrada house, rubbing his big fist.

After staying more than a week in Dr. Enquito Estrada's house, Wolf Bixler and his group rode out under cover of darkness just before dawn. Josefina was feeling much better, and the sparkle was returning to her eyes. The doctor warned Rosa to dress her warmly at all times and to keep her dry.

Armand still bore the marks of his beating, but the swelling in his lips was gone, and he could smile without pain. From his place at the rear of the column, he looked past Diego Corral and his sister to the massive man on the big sorrel. Warmth flooded through the young man. Wolf Bixler was not only his hero but had proven to be his friend.

Smiling to himself, Armand thought of the beating Wolf had given Luis Arguello. The man's woman friend had brought him to Dr. Estrada's clinic the morning after Wolf had administered the punishment. While the others remained in their rooms, Armand had sneaked in and stolen a look at Luis as he was leaving the clinic after treatment. His face was so swollen, he did not look like the same man.

After Arguello and his woman friend had gone, Dr. Estrada had told his house guests that the bully had a broken nose and a broken jaw. Both lips were split so badly they required stitches. Arguello had described his assailant as seven feet tall and weighing four hundred pounds, saying he was half animal and half man.

Armand enjoyed the warm glow inside him. Wolf was the best friend he had ever had. The youth was entertaining thoughts of asking Wolf if he could live with him, once Rosa and Josefina were safe in San Antonio with Dido Gomez. He figured it would be really great to live with Wolf. He could learn to fight. Armand could never be as big as his friend, but Wolf could help him become strong and tough. Wolf could teach him how to use a revolver better, too. And how to throw a knife.

Moving once again through open country, the travelers were able to ride abreast. Conversation between Rosa, Armand, and Diego was of San Antonio, Dido Gomez, and safety from Díaz. Rosa and Armand spoke of their father, wondering if he had made it safely to Acapulco. Would he ever be able to meet them in San Antonio?

Armand told himself even if his father *did* make it safely to San Antonio, he 'wanted to live with Wolf Bixler.

At midday, Pedro Llamas pointed out the town of San Juan del Rio in the distance to the west. They had now come just over a hundred miles from Mexico City.

As they rode on, conversation between brother and sister also included their departed mother, sister, and brother-in-law. Silent tears were shed by both.

Late in the afternoon, while beginning to look for a good camping spot, Wolf Bixler pulled his horse alongside Diego's, which also carried Josefina. She smiled at the big man, calling him Uncle Wolf. Again he reminded her that she was not his niece.

The sleepy mountain village of San Rosario was stirred two days after the travelers had bid the Estradas goodbye. Seven riders thundered into the village at noon, dressed in tan uniforms. They drew up in front of the cantina in a cloud of dust.

San Rosario's residents looked on in silent intimidation as Captain Alex Bisera and his men dismounted. The common people of Mexico did not like the Federales; their presence always meant trouble.

Bisera, a short, stout man with inflexible black eyes, led his men into the cool, dark interior of the cantina. Shoving two tables together, they scraped chairs on the wooden floor and sat down.

Onzo Pinza, the elderly proprietor, came from behind the bar, visibly nervous, and asked the men their pleasure. Returning to the Federales with a bottle of his best whiskey and seven glasses on a tray, he distributed the glasses, set the bottle in front of Bisera, and turned to leave.

"Hold on, old man," said the captain, grasping his arm. "We are looking for a man. An escaped criminal. It is possible he has passed through your village."

"I have not seen him," Pinza said, shaking his head.

"How do you know?" asked Bisera, tightening his grip on the old man's arm. "I have not yet described him!"

Onzo swallowed hard, unable to pull his fearful gaze from the captain's unrelenting eyes.

"This criminal is a gringo," said Bisera. "A giant of a man. Big and strong. Wears a heavy beard. His name is Wolf Bixler. He is mean like a wild beast."

Onzo Pinza immediately thought of Luis Arguello's assailant. Everyone in the village had heard about the fight. Forcing a smile, he said, "Sí. Sí. There was such a man here one or two weeks ago. He beat up on an hombre named Luis Arguello."

Bisera grinned, patting the arm he had gripped so hard. "Now that is what I like to hear. My men and I will have a little drink, and then you will tell us where we can find this Luis Arguello."

Five days passed without incident. The travelers were finding the ground more level as they pressed northward, and by riding from sunup to sundown, they were now able to cover twenty miles a day. The air was getting warmer as they dropped in elevation.

As the procession topped a gentle rise in late morning, Pedro Llamas drew rein, and the others pulled abreast. A bustling town spread out below them. It was the largest town they had seen since leaving Mexico City.

"That is Ciudad Victoria," Pedro advised the others. "We are now almost three hundred miles from Mexico City. We will need to replenish our supplies here."

Wolf Bixler remembered passing through Ciudad Victoria on his trip with Gilbert Salazar.

Pedro led them into a wooded area where they could rest until he and Diego returned from town. As the two Mexicans were riding away with the packhorse, Wolf called out to Pedro, telling him to stay away from the cantinas. Pedro lifted his hat as signal that he had heard and could be trusted to obey.

In less than half an hour, the group saw the two men returning, followed by the packhorse. Wolf walked toward them as they pulled up. "What's wrong?" he asked, knowing they were back too soon.

Diego dismounted, flashing his pearly white teeth in a smile. Armand, Rosa, and Josefina came close.

"We have lost track of time on this trip," Diego said. "This is Christmas Day. The businesses are all closed."

"Christmas Day!" exclaimed Rosa.

Josefina clapped her hands, jumping up and down. "Merry Christmas!" she shouted. "Merry Christmas to everybody!"

Wolf decided they would rest for the remainder of the day. They were low on provisions and had to wait until they could stock up in Ciudad Victoria on the morrow. The group made camp and built a fire in the wooded area.

Josefina gathered pinecones, took them to the spot where her own things were laid out, and sat down on a fallen tree. Opening her satchel, she took out a length of red ribbon she had brought along to make bows for her hair. Cutting the ribbon into five pieces, she tied each one to a pinecone.

The task completed, Josefina carried a cone to her

aunt. Childish light danced in her eyes as she handed it to her saying, "Merry Christmas, Aunt Rosa."

Tears brimmed Rosa Tejada's eyes as she accepted the gift, embracing Josefina, kissing her. She remembered the Christmas before, when the family was together in the presidential mansion. Now the little girl had no parents with whom to share the joy of the season.

Josefina carried cones to Armand, Diego, and Pedro, and with each one she gave and received a hug and a kiss.

When she approached the big bearded man, her black eyes danced with delight. Wolf was seated on the ground cross-legged. She handed him the ribbon-adorned pinecone and said, "Merry Christmas, Uncle Wolf. I love you."

Wolf moistened his lips nervously. Josefina had him off balance again. He had braced himself for the inevitable hug and kiss the child would give him when she came with her gift; he had weathered several of her hugs before. And he figured he could withstand a kiss on his cheek. But Josefina had rattled him hard this time, by saying three words no one had ever spoken to him in his entire life. Indians were not expressive in that way, and in the years since leaving the Comanches, Wolf had encountered anything but love.

Wolf decided he would not reprimand Josefina for calling him uncle this time. After all, it was Christmas. He had heard somewhere that you were supposed to be kind to people on Christmas. He wondered if this was not sentimentality working on him, however.

Rosa observed the big man's discomfort. Massive in size, oxlike in strength, Wolf Bixler could take on five Mexican bandits singlehandedly and kill them, but he could not handle the tenderness and love of a gentle, sweet little girl.

At Josefina's *I love you*, Rosa thought she saw the faint hint of a smile tug at the corners of the big man's mouth. It vanished as the child threw her arms around his neck. And then Rosa saw something else. While Josefina was embracing him, Wolf's big hands started upward to fold around her. Rosa's heart leaped. Suddenly Wolf checked himself, dropping his hands and muttering something indistinguishable.

Rosa had to turn her head away to hide the smile that broke across her lips. Slowly, but surely, Josefina Montoya was breaking down Wolf Bixler's resistance.

After breakfast on December 26, 1876, Diego Corral and Pedro Llamas rode into Ciudad Victoria for food and supplies.

Entering the large general store, they moved about, picking up items and carrying them to the counter. They noticed a tall, slender gringo come in, but paid him no mind.

The tall man was scooping pinto beans from an open barrel into a cloth bag when he heard Pedro say to Diego, "I wish Wolf Bixler could have come with us to town. He could carry this hundred-pound sack of cornmeal to the packhorse with one hand."

Stuart Jarrell's ears perked up. He turned away quickly so they would not see his badge.

Chapter Thirteen

Dawn came, staining the eastern sky with dull gray light.

United States marshal Stuart Jarrell had waited until now to make his play. He would capture his man this morning and have the rest of the day to ride. In his coat pocket were two pairs of handcuffs. One might not be enough to hold the powerful outlaw.

Observing the camp from the surrounding thicket, it was not hard for Jarrell to tell which bedroll contained Wolf Bixler. Beside him were the bedrolls of four others. The small form had to be a child. He wondered why Wolf Bixler was camping with these men. No outlaw gang would take along a child.

The marshal's plan was to wait in the shadows until Wolf Bixler got up. As with all mortals, Wolf would have to relieve his bladder after a night's sleep, and Jarrell was gambling he would move off into the woods to take care of it. There he would be vulnerable, and Jarrell would get the drop on him. Whoever the other men were, they would not want any shooting with a child in the camp.

Jarrell's heart quickened pace when he saw the large form on the ground begin stirring. Within seconds, Wolf Bixler stood up, stretched, and yawned. The marshal waited expectantly for Wolf to head into the woods, but instead he began building a fire.

Suddenly Jarrell saw movement in the thicket on the

opposite side of the camp. There was a noise like thunder, and Wolf Bixler went diving for his guns, which lay by his bedroll.

Seven Federales broke through the heavy timber on horseback, guns drawn. A revolver roared, and the bullet chewed ground where Wolf was reaching. The big man froze on the spot.

"Do not even think of reaching for those guns, Señor Bixler!" shouted the leader. "You do, and you die!"

The rest of the camp was awake now. Marshal Stuart Jarrell pulled back into the shadows and watched. He saw that one of the sleeping forms had been a woman . . . a very beautiful woman.

The dark-skinned Federales sat on their horses in tan uniforms with black belts and holsters supported by single black shoulder straps angling across their chests. They wore black boots and small-billed caps that matched their uniforms.

Their leader dismounted, eyeing those who sat on the ground, still in their bedrolls. Swaggering about, he said, "I am Captain Alexander Bisera of the federal police. Each of you on the ground is a *mejicano*. Why would you run with the likes of a dirty gringo killer like Bixler? Or did you not know that he had escaped from the federal prison at Mexico City? He was to be hanged for murdering *mejicanos!*"

Wolf spoke up, "These people are not my companions, Captain. I only came upon them last night and begged a meal from them. They were kind enough to let me spend the night in their camp."

Bisera swung his hard gaze to Rosa Tejada. "Is this true, señorita?" he asked.

Rosa detested lying, but at this point it was necessary. "Sí, Captain," she answered.

"Which way are you traveling?" Bisera demanded.

"North, Captain," Rosa replied. "To Nuevo Laredo."

Bisera accepted Rosa's word. Raking Armand, Diego, and Pedro with his dark gaze, he said, "We will now relieve you of your guest. He is going back to prison, where he will hang."

Rosa was about to panic, but knew better than to

show it. The Federales were going to take Wolf away, and there was nothing she or the others could do about it.

Waving his revolver at Wolf, Bisera said, "You may put your coat on, señor. You will get your horse and make ready to ride." Chuckling, he added, "We were getting worried, Bixler. Tomorrow was the last day we could apprehend you. We have orders from Porfirio Díaz to return to Mexico City by the tenth day of January. If we had not found you in time to turn around and make it to Mexico City by then, we were to give up the pursuit."

A grim look of gloom showed in Wolf Bixler's dark eyes.

While the big man saddled his horse under heavy guard, the captain picked up the twin bandoliers and double-holstered gun belt from beside his blankets. Wolf rolled up his bedding and tied it to the back of the saddle.

Waving his gun in a cocky manner, Bisera told Wolf to mount up. When he was settled in the saddle, the captain nodded to two of his men, and quickly they slipped to the ground and dug in their saddlebags, producing wrist chains and leg irons. Locking the leg irons around Wolf's boots at the ankles, they connected them under the horse's belly with a three-foot length of chain and then shackled his wrists in front of him.

Cold sweat moistened Wolf's brow. Chained the way he was, escape was impossible. He thought of having to climb the gallow steps and face the noose again.

Bisera looped the bandolier belts on his own shoulders and stuffed the double-holstered gun belt in his saddlebag. Swinging aboard his mount, he said, "All right, señor *mejicano* killer, let us ride."

Wolf wanted to look back at his little group of companions but knew he couldn't take the chance. Bisera might suspect that he was more than an overnight guest in their camp.

As the Federales and their prisoner passed from view in the dense forest, Armand Tejada leaped to his feet. Wild-eyed, he said to Diego, "Come on! We must find a way to rescue Wolf!" Turning to Pedro, he gasped, "We have to do something fast!"

"What can we do?" asked Pedro, climbing out of his bedroll.

"We have to think of something," Diego spoke up. "We cannot let them take Señor Wolf back to be hanged."

Rosa emerged from her blankets, smoothed her clothes, and brushed at her hair. Her eyes were pinched with fear. "We must go after them," she said. "It will not be easy, but we must find a way to take Wolf from the Federales."

"I will be glad to help," came a strange voice from the shadow of the trees.

All eyes swerved to the owner of the voice as he walked toward them. He was broad-shouldered and had a jawline that spoke of dogged determination. His steel-gray eyes accentuated it. "I am United States marshal Stuart Jarrell," the man said.

At that instant they all noticed his badge.

"I assume Mr. Bixler really is more to you people than a beggar who spent the night," Jarrell said, looking into Rosa's eyes.

"Yes," she answered. "Señor Wolf was taking us to San Antonio."

"San Antonio?" echoed the marshal. He found the Mexican woman's beauty captivating.

"You have heard of our revolution problems in Mexico?" queried Rosa.

"Yes." Jarrell nodded. "I have heard that Porfirio Díaz has deposed President Tejada and is seeking to kill him."

"Yes," said the lovely señorita. "And Díaz is also seeking to kill El Presidente Tejada's children and granddaughter. I am Rosa Tejada. This is my brother, Armand Tejada, and this little girl is our niece, Josefina Montoya."

Stuart Jarrell stood dumbfounded for a minute. Rosa introduced Diego Corral and Pedro Llamas to him and then told him their story, from Wolf Bixler's arranged escape to the present.

Jarrell realized, then, that it was a sheer stroke of luck that he had encountered Wolf Bixler.

"Marshal Jarrell," Diego said, "you indicated you would help us get Señor Wolf back. Are we to understand that you make this offer because you want to place him under arrest?"

Jarrell answered in the affirmative and then told his own story. "You will agree," he concluded, "that it is better for Bixler to go back with me. At least he will live if he does. There is no death sentence against him in Texas. We both want to rescue him from the Federales. While I am taking him back, we will also get you safely to San Antonio. Shall we work together?"

Little Josefina, a silent spectator to all the events of the morning, said worriedly, "Rosa, I do not want the bad men to take Uncle Wolf away."

Rosa assured the child that Marshal Jarrell was going to help them get Uncle Wolf back from the bad men.

While Rosa cooked breakfast, the men worked out their plan. Jarrell was going to exclude Armand from the rescue team until Diego told him that the youth was quite capable with a gun.

"What we need to do," said the marshal, "is ride around them, find the right spot, and surprise them. We'll need to position ourselves so they're pinned in a crossfire."

It was decided that Rosa and Josefina would remain at the camp, and as soon as they finished breakfast, Marshal Jarrell and the three Mexicans rode south in pursuit of the Federales.

Bitterness welled up strong within Wolf Bixler as he rode toward Mexico City, shackled and surrounded by Federales. Not only was he bitter about his own predicament, but it grated him that Rosa, Armand, and Josefina were left with a perilous journey and little protection.

Diego would do his best, even to laying down his life for the three exiles, but he was no fighter. Pedro would probably be more protection for them, except he had not demonstrated that much personal concern for their safety. He was liable to find a cantina somewhere, get drunk, and desert them.

Wolf figured that if it came right down to it, the best fighter in the bunch would be Armand. The kid had spunk. What he lacked in experience, he would make up in grit.

". . . that you did not make it, Bixler." Captain Bisera was riding beside Wolf, and his words had intruded into the big man's thoughts.

Wolf turned and asked, "What'd you say?"

"I said I am glad you did not make it, señor," Bisera repeated. "It would have been a shame to let you get away. Señor Porfirio Díaz is aware that you killed his loyal followers, the Salazars. He is eager to see you at the end of a rope. He will also reward me handsomely for bringing you back."

"What if we don't make it to Mexico City by the tenth?"

Wolf saw the trepidation in Bisera's eyes. Díaz was a tyrant, and his orders were to be obeyed explicitly; to fail was to die.

Bisera pulled his lips into a thin line. "We will make it, señor," he retorted.

They were riding two abreast, climbing a steep slope through scented clumps of pine and winding around massive boulders. The white-surfaced rocks were awash with the morning's bright sunlight. As they topped the slope, they were flanked on both sides by twelve-foot-high boulders.

Suddenly a tall, rawboned figure appeared on the boulder to the right. The Federales stiffened in their saddles, reaching for their revolvers. But they froze before touching their guns.

To their left were two more men, and another stepped out of the pine shadows to their right flank. The Federales were locked in a dangerous crossfire.

Though Wolf Bixler was surprised to see his old nemesis Stuart Jarrell, he had never been so glad to see a lawman in all his life.

"Hello, Wolf." Jarrell grinned.

"What is this?" demanded Captain Alex Bisera.

"I guess you'd call it a rescue, Captain," answered the marshal, his badge gleaming in the sunlight. "I was about to move in on Bixler this morning, when you and your boys beat me to it."

"You cannot do this!" Bisera blared. "Bixler is a prisoner of the Mexican government!"

"He was a prisoner of the United States government first," Jarrell said coolly, training the muzzle of his cocked Colt .44 on the captain's chest. "He's up on a manslaughter charge in Waco. Broke out of prison. I'm taking him back."

Wolf looked around at Armand, who stood at the right flank, gun in hand. The youthful face broke into a wide smile. Though Wolf's lips did not curve, there was the shadow of gratification in his eyes.

From their position on the left, Diego and Pedro held their guns steady.

"You are an officer of the law," reasoned the flustered captain. "You will not shoot us!"

Determination sparkled in Stuart Jarrell's eyes. "I will if I have to, Captain. Don't make me prove it." His words were as sharp and jagged as broken glass.

Bisera's swarthy face was shiny with sweat. He was about to lose his prisoner. There would be no handsome reward from Díaz.

"Armand," said the marshal, "relieve the Federales of their guns. Don't forget the prisoner's weapons in the captain's saddlebags."

The youth fulfilled his task gladly, also taking the bandoliers from Bisera's shoulders.

Jarrell set his firm gaze on the shackled man. "Now, Wolf," he said, "we can do this one of two ways. I know you, and I know with all your faults you are a man of your word. It's more than four hundred miles to San Antonio. You want to get your group there safely. We could face many obstacles between here and there. I want to get you to Waco. So—"

"So you want my word that if you let me out of these chains and give me back my guns, I'll surrender myself to you when we get to San Antonio," he cut in.

"You got it," came Jarrell's dry reply.

Wolf knew he had no choice. Anything was better than stretching a rope in that Mexican prison, and he needed his guns in order to meet any emergency along the way. The only problem was that he would need a few days to get the gold from Dido Gomez and deliver it to Chief Iron Face once they got to San Antonio.

"Well?" Jarrell said.

"I have some very important business to handle when we get to San Antonio," Wolf replied. "Will you give me a week before I surrender to you at Waco?"

The marshal considered it for a brief moment. "Okay," he said. "If you'll give me your word that you will turn yourself in to me at Waco one week from the day we arrive in San Antonio, I'll take you out of those chains and give you your guns back."

"You have my word on it," Wolf said firmly.

Within three minutes the shackles were removed and Wolf had the Colt .45s on his hips and the bandoliers crisscrossed on his chest.

Captain Alex Bisera looked ill as Marshal Stuart Jarrell and the four men rode away with the Federales' weapons. The best he could hope for now was to make it to Mexico City by the deadline date. Maybe he could talk his men into lying to Díaz for him. The ruthless dictator would be much easier on him if his compadres corroborated his story that Wolf Bixler had simply eluded them.

Rosa Tejada was elated to see the men return with Wolf Bixler, as was little Josefina.

Stuart Jarrell told Rosa about the pact he and Wolf had made, and though she hated the thought of Wolf having to return to the Waco prison, she was relieved that he would escape the noose in Mexico City.

Pedro Llamas led the group across Mexico's rugged terrain as the days and miles were left behind. Many canyons were interlaced among the eastern slopes of the Sierra Madres, and Pedro knew when to skirt them and when to use them as passageways to hasten their trek toward the Texas border.

United States marshal Stuart Jarrell found that his
thoughts of Peggy Garner were fading away the more
he was around Rosa Tejada. She was capturing his
heart.

The travelers were camped on the edge of a deep
canyon about two weeks after Jarrell had joined them.
Night had fallen. Everyone except the marshal had
slipped into their bedrolls. There was a nip in the night
air, and the moon and stars were brilliant in the crystal
clear sky.

From her bedroll, Rosa saw Jarrell walk to the brink
of the canyon. She watched his tall shape, outlined
against the dazzling January sky. In the last two weeks
they had shared many talks, discussing the revolution
in Mexico, her father's loss of power, and his subsequent exile. The beautiful señorita had told him of her
happy childhood, the love in her home, and the grief
she felt in losing her mother, sister, and brother-in-law.

As she watched him walk along the canyon's rim and
pondered their talks together, she suddenly realized
how little he had spoken of himself. He had given her a
brief sketch of his job as Waco's town marshal and told
her of his recent appointment as a federal lawman. But
nothing about his personal life had been mentioned,
and there had been nothing said about any female
relationships.

Rosa was finding herself extremely attracted to the
tall man—more attracted, in fact, than she had ever
been to a man. She lay there watching him while the
others slept, Josefina asleep beside her, breathing evenly.

Curiosity, coupled with some unfamiliar inward force,
compelled Rosa to rise from her blankets. She felt the
soft breeze from the canyon touch her face as she
slipped into her leather jacket and walked toward the
tall figure at the chasm's edge.

Stuart Jarrell heard the soft footsteps coming from
behind. Looking away from the moonlit depths of the
canyon, he turned to see the beautiful young woman
smiling at him. He smiled in return. "Hello."

"Lovely night," she breathed, running her eyes across
the shimmering sky.

"Sure is. Mexico is almost as beautiful as Texas."

Without commenting, Rosa asked, "What were you thinking about?"

Jarrell felt his face tint. "Oh, a couple things."

"Home?"

"No," he answered, turning to peer at the spread of dark mountains across the chasm.

"I assume you have a home."

"I have a *house* in Waco. It takes more than that to make a home."

Rosa's heart quickened pace. "There is no woman in your life, Stu?"

"No."

Rosa was quiet for a moment. Then she asked, "Have you ever been in love?"

"Yes . . . well, I thought I had until . . ."

"Until what?"

The tough man was like butter in Rosa Tejada's presence. He turned to look at her. The silver moonlight enhanced her exquisite beauty, and the breeze toyed with her hair. "Rosa . . ."

"Yes?" Her voice was soft as silk.

"That morning I walked into the camp and first laid eyes on you . . ."

"Yes?"

"Something happened inside me. I can't explain it. Up until a few days ago, I didn't know what it was. But now . . ."

Rosa's heart was drumming against her ribs. "Stu," she said, moving closer to him, "something happened inside me that morning, too."

They stood looking at each other in the moonlight, words no longer necessary. He reached out and pulled Rosa to him, and their lips came together in a lingering, tender kiss.

"Oh, Rosa," he sighed, as she laid her head against his throbbing chest. Holding her tight, he said, "You asked me what I was thinking about."

"Mmm-hmm."

"Two things."

"Yes?"

"How utterly beautiful you are, and how very much I love you. I . . . I was trying to figure out a way to tell you."

Lifting her face toward his, she said softly, "Then tell me."

"I love you, Rosa."

The silver light from the Mexican sky caught the adoration in her eyes as she looked up at him. "I love you too, my Stuart," she breathed warmly, and again their lips met.

Sweeping streaks of red ran across the eastern sky as the Texas-bound travelers swung into their saddles. Looking at Bixler, Pedro Llamas said, "We will cut around this canyon to the north, señor. Then we will have to drop down and pass through the next one. It will save us about thirty miles."

"Fine with me." The big bearded man nodded. "Let's go."

Wolf guided his horse past the spot where Josefina sat in the saddle with Diego Corral. The bright-eyed child gave him a wide smile.

Rosa and Jarrell flashed each other a furtive grin, enjoying their secret love.

Two hours brought the column of riders to the brink of the canyon Pedro had said they would pass through. A narrow path descended into the chasm, zigzagging its way down the face of the vast wall like a long snake.

Entering the path single file, they inched their way down the steep decline, Pedro in the lead, followed by Wolf. Behind him came Rosa and then the marshal, who was followed by Diego and Josefina. Armand brought up the rear, leading the packhorse.

It took them over an hour to reach the bottom of the canyon. They followed Pedro along a dry wash, the sheer granite walls looming high above them.

Presently, they came to where a waterfall cascaded down a gray canyon wall from a hundred feet up. At the bottom was a sparkling pool where the water paused momentarily before falling into an unseen aperture, where it plunged deeper into the earth's bowels.

"We will rest here a few minutes," Pedro declared as they drew up to the pool. "We can fill up the canteens and water the horses well."

With delight, Josefina discovered that the bottom of the pool was covered with small shiny stones that seemed to change colors with the water's movement. She hailed everybody to come and see them. When she called Bixler "Uncle Wolf," he reminded her once again with a grumble that he was not her uncle.

While Josefina had the group clustered in a semicircle at the pool, Pedro backed away unnoticed. He pulled his holstered revolver and drew a small .32 caliber pistol from his coat.

Suddenly his voice slashed through the canyon's stillness. "Everybody stay right where you are! Get your hands toward the sky!"

Chapter Fourteen

Breathing heavily, Pedro Llamas stood with guns aimed, his cheeks flushed with the threat of violence.

"Armand!" he barked as they all raised their hands. "Get everybody's guns and put them in my saddlebags!"

The youth hesitated, looking at Wolf Bixler.

"Now!" Pedro bellowed.

"Do it, boy," Wolf said softly.

Armand began collecting guns, but he was not moving fast enough to suit the guide. "Hurry up!" Pedro snarled. His heavy breathing revealed his anxiety. He had been waiting for this moment for a long time.

As Armand gathered the guns with his back to Pedro, he pulled Rosa's .38 from its holster and slipped it under his belt, covering the butt with his coat. He carried the other weapons to Pedro's horse and deposited them in the saddlebags.

Gesturing toward an open area to his right, Pedro said, "Get over there, Armand. Pull your coat up so I can see your holster."

Armand lifted his coat just enough to show the desperate Mexican that the holster was empty, but without revealing Rosa's gun.

One by one, Pedro made the group step toward Armand, showing him their empty holsters. Josefina hovered close to Rosa, whimpering in fright.

Wolf Bixler was the last person at the pool, and he glared maliciously at the stout-bodied Mexican.

"Do not even think it, Bixler," warned Pedro. "You would never have a chance to get your hands on me." Motioning with his head, he said, "Get over there with the rest of them!"

Puzzled by Pedro's strange action, Rosa's voice cracked as she said to him, "Pedro, what are you doing? What does all this mean?"

As Wolf stepped near Rosa, he answered for the guide. "What it means, girl, is that this dirty snake in the grass has led us into a trap. He works for Díaz."

Wolf observed the alarm that froze Rosa and kept her from speaking. The faces of Diego and Armand went slack with horror, and Stuart Jarrell stiffened.

Pedro smiled wickedly with thin lips. In a voice cool and threatening, he said, "You are very smart for a gringo, Bixler. How did you know?"

"Simple," mumbled Wolf. "You're standin' there holdin' those guns on us, aren't you? Why else would you be doing that? We haven't got enough money among us for you to be robbin' us. So you've got some pals close by, right? And together you've planned an execution, right?"

Rosa gasped. Her eyes were wide with fear. Jarrell moved next to her and placed his arm around her shoulders, while Josefina stood clinging to her waist.

"You really are smart, gringo." Pedro chuckled wickedly. "My *compañeros* are waiting for us. When they look this way, they will see us and come running. In the meantime, if you want to try something, please do. It would be my pleasure to put a bullet in your heart."

"Pedro," Diego spoke up, "why have you done this thing? El Presidente trusted you."

"El Presidente," Pedro said, curling his upper lip, "is a *pig!*" With that, he spat on the ground.

Anger lanced through Armand's body. He wanted to use the gun under his coat, but he knew Pedro would shoot him down before he could pull the trigger. He had to bide his time and choose the right moment. If only he could slip the gun to Wolf . . .

"Since we have a few moments, I will tell you why I

did it," Pedro said, holding the guns steady. "I was approached by a man in Tejada's cabinet named Ben Vomero. He told me that El Presidente was going to send Rosa and Armand to Dido Gomez in San Antonio. He needed a man who knows the country to guide them on the journey. Vomero offered me ten thousand dollars in gold if I would take the job and lead them to Díaz's men in this canyon."

"No!" Rosa screamed, her eyes bulging. "Ben Vomero is one of my father's loyal, trusted men!"

Pedro laughed. "Trusted, yes. Your father is a fool! Loyal, no. Ben Vomero sold out to Porfirio Díaz months ago. It was because your father trusted Ben that this worked out so well. He told El Presidente that I was trustworthy for this job, so I got it."

"Was not my father going to pay you for guiding us?" Rosa queried.

Laughing again, Pedro said, "Sí, he did pay me. But nowhere near ten thousand dollars."

Shaking her head, Rosa said, "It is so hard to believe this about Ben. Why would he turn against my father?"

"Simple." Pedro grinned. "Money. One of Díaz's top guerrilla leaders is Aldo Vomero, Ben's brother. Aldo saw to it that Ben was paid well for providing information. Aldo is wanting to be appointed to a high government position in Díaz's new regime, and he is certain to attain it if he delivers you and your brother and the muchacha to Díaz for execution. And since I brought you to Aldo, he will not only give me the gold, but he will get me a high-paying job, too!"

Rosa looked at him with disbelief. "And it does not bother you to see us executed?"

The guide hunched his shoulders. "A man has to make a living," he said tonelessly.

Her face set with consternation, Rosa asked, "Why did you bother to jump in the river that day and try to rescue Josefina?"

Pedro chuckled. "My orders are to deliver all three of you to Aldo Vomero. Señor Díaz wants the privilege of personally eliminating every living relative of Tejada.

Besides, my little act of heroism kept any suspicion away from me, no?"

Wolf Bixler's eyes burned with savagery. "I'll get my hands on you sooner or later," he exploded.

"It will have to be later!" Pedro laughed. "My friends are here now!"

Six dark-skinned, mean-looking Mexican men came thundering in on horseback. At gunpoint, they forced their prisoners to walk a quarter mile deeper into the canyon and then herded them into a large cave. It was Aldo Vomero's hideout.

Pedro Llamas told Wolf and the others that Vomero had an army of thirty guerrillas. One of the six present spoke up and said that Vomero and the twenty-four others were gone at the moment. They would be back later.

The six guerrillas observed Rosa with wanton eyes. Stuart Jarrell glared at them, and Josefina clung to Rosa's hand. Armand was hoping for a chance to slip Wolf the gun.

The prisoners were ushered deep into the cave, which was well lighted with lanterns. They were amazed to see hundreds of ammunition crates and a large supply of rifles and revolvers. A covered wagon was parked near the crates, and as they moved past the rear of the wagon, where they could see inside it, Wolf Bixler's eyes bulged.

Mounted in the covered wagon was a brand-new, shiny 1876 model Gatling gun. Wolf eyed its ten .58 caliber muzzles, housed in a perfect circle within the tubular steel casing. He thought of Chief Iron Face and what the Comanches could do if they had that powerful machine of death.

Still holding their prisoners at gunpoint, the six guerrillas and Pedro Llamas crowded them next to a rock wall in the cave. A hostile-looking Mexican named Victorio Mendosa seemed to be in charge.

Pedro slid his revolver into its holster and told Mendosa and the others of the proposed rendezvous the group had with Dido Gomez at the Alamo in San

Antonio. Laughing, he said, "Gomez will be old and gray by the time he figures out they are not coming!"

The guerrillas joined in the merriment.

Laughing still harder, Pedro said, "I cannot wait until Aldo comes and pays me my gold. I am going to get stinking drunk now!"

Victorio Mendosa laughed hollowly with Pedro and then deliberately leveled his gun on the guide's belly. "You are to be paid for your trouble *before* Aldo returns," he said in a cold, icy voice.

Pedro's laughter choked off instantly, the broad smile that had accompanied the laughter fading away. He looked at the threatening gun and then lifted fearful eyes to Mendosa's dark, granite face. With a tremulous voice, he said, "You make a joke, no?"

"No joke," Mendosa rasped. "It is Aldo's belief that a man who will turn traitor for money once will do it again."

Pedro's face was sallow, with fear etched around his mouth. Like a whimpering child, he began begging for his life, trembling.

While Pedro continued to grovel, Wolf Bixler and Stuart Jarrell were each trying to think of a way to overpower the six guerrillas. Once Aldo and his full force arrived, all hope of escape would be gone.

Josefina was clinging to both Rosa and Diego, sensing the violence that was about to erupt.

The six guerrillas watched Pedro, who was on his knees, weeping, begging for mercy. They did not notice Armand inching his way along the rock wall, moving apart from the others. He slowly was positioning himself behind the six men.

Pedro's wailing filled the cave, and Victorio Mendosa was enjoying the traitor's agony. He placed the muzzle of his cocked revolver an inch from Pedro's upturned face, aiming it between his terror-filled eyes. The other five guerrillas looked on with delight, their complete attention on the terrified man.

Both Wolf and Jarrell had noticed Armand, who was now behind the guerrillas. Neither had any idea what the boy was up to, but there was no way to stop him.

Their muscles tense, they poised themselves, ready to act regardless of what happened.

"Adios, traitor," Mendosa said with a wicked smile, and pulled the trigger.

The gun roared, and a black hole appeared between Pedro Llamas's eyes. His body flipped backward from the bullet's impact.

While the shot was clattering in a deafening echo off the walls of the cave and Josefina was screaming, Armand fired the .38 revolver in his hand. The slug ripped through Mendosa's head; he was dead before his own smoking gun slipped from his fingers. The noise of the second shot joined the clamor of the first along the cave walls.

Like a seasoned veteran, Armand then swung the muzzle on the five guerrillas, holding it steady with both hands. The hammer was eared back. "Drop your guns!" he bellowed.

At the same instant, Wolf Bixler dived for Mendosa's revolver, and Stuart Jarrell made a plunge for the gun in Pedro's holster.

The five guerrillas reacted to the movement of the two men, bringing their guns to bear, and one fired at Wolf. Armand's revolver boomed repeatedly, striking down three of them. Wolf seized Mendosa's gun from the cave's floor, rolled to dodge a bullet, and shot the man who had just fired at him. The bullet had missed Wolf by less than an inch.

The U.S. marshal whipped Pedro's gun from its holster in time to shoot one of the men Armand had already dropped. The man, though mortally wounded, was attempting to raise his gun on Wolf.

The remaining guerrilla stumbled and then turned to fire at Armand. The youth fired first, putting his last bullet in the man's heart.

Josefina's voice was now frozen with fright, and the echo of the last shot died out in the cave unaccompanied by her screams.

Fanning the blue-white gun smoke from his face, Wolf turned to Armand. "That was some shootin', boy. You just saved our lives. Where'd you get that gun?"

"It's Rosa's," responded the youth, sweat covering his face. "I slipped it under my belt when I took it from her holster."

Everyone congratulated Armand for his swift thinking and his courage. Diego apologized that he had not entered into the gunfight, but explained that there were no more guns to dive for until it was all over. Laughing, Stuart Jarrell patted him on the back, saying Diego would probably get the chance to display his courage before this journey was over.

"We'd better get out of here fast," said Wolf. "Aldo and his army will be showin' up." Swinging his gaze toward the covered wagon, he added, "Let's take the Gatling with us."

Knowing Aldo Vomero's army might follow them, marshal Stuart Jarrell agreed. He asked Wolf if he could operate the Gatling, and the big man gave an affirmative answer, while heading for a horse team he had noticed outside the cave. They were in a rope corral with several saddle horses.

Diego helped Wolf harness the team while Jarrell handed weapons and ammunition to Armand, who was in the covered wagon. As Armand moved about in the wagon, he said, "Señor Stu, there are tools in here. Shovels, picks, axes, and some rope. Shall I throw them out?"

Jarrell looked to see how many there were. "No, just leave them there," he answered.

Wolf climbed into the wagon and examined the Gatling gun. It was loaded and ready to fire. "Okay, Stu," he said. "There's a stack of ammunition boxes over there. Let's load them all in the wagon."

While this was being done, Diego and Rosa left the cave to round up the group's horses.

When the wagon was loaded and the horses had been harnessed to it, Wolf climbed into the seat and took the reins. Clucking at the horses, he drove the heavily laden vehicle out into the sunshine, Wolf's and Rosa's horses tied behind. Josefina sat with Rosa and Wolf in the wagon seat, and Jarrell and Diego flanked the wagon. Armand followed behind, leading the packhorse.

As the travelers made their way toward the mouth of the canyon, Diego pulled his horse close to the wagon and said, "Señor Wolf, should we have blown up the cave with the rest of the ammunition that is back there?"

"I thought of it," Wolf replied, "but if the other guerrillas are near, the noise would bring them runnin'."

Diego nodded and moved back to his flanking position.

Riding at the rear, Armand still felt shaky inside, but there was also a warm glow in his breast. He had saved their lives. Wolf Bixler's compliment had added fuel to the warmth he was feeling.

The covered wagon was wheeled out of the mouth of the canyon, heading northward across a broad, sweeping valley. Giant rock formations dotted the valley floor, along with scattered clusters of brush and piñon trees. On the far side of the valley were more rugged mountains, engulfed at the moment in a blue haze.

As the wagon rumbled over the relatively level ground, the travelers noticed a huge rock shaped like a castle, even to four cone-shaped towers and several crude, weather-beaten parapets. Josefina commented on the bizarre formation, but Wolf Bixler's mind was on the Gatling gun. He had to get it to Iron Face at all costs.

Rosa Tejada let her eyes rest on the tall, angular man who rode his horse on her side of the wagon. She breathed a prayer of thanks that both of them were still alive. Somehow they had to make it through to San Antonio. Now that they had found each other, they could not allow anything to stop them from having a life together.

Jarrell pulled close to the wagon, pointing at a cloud of dust to the east. Wolf followed Jarrell's finger with his dark eyes, and Rosa gasped. It was a band of riders.

"Guerrillas!" shouted Diego, who had just spotted them.

Wolf swore. Squinting to focus on the galloping riders, he counted the dark figures against the background of buff-colored dust. "Looks like about fifteen or so," he said to the others. "Part of Aldo's army is headed for the cave. They've seen us! They know we're stealin' the wagon!"

There was about a mile between the travelers and the charging guerrillas.

Wolf set the brake and leaped into the back of the wagon. While he pulled the canvas cover from the arched ribs, he said to Rosa, "Take the little one, get on your horse, and ride back to that castle-shaped rock. Take my horse with you. Hurry!"

As Rosa scrambled out of the wagon, taking Josefina with her, Wolf shouted at Armand, "Boy! Go with your sister!"

"But you will need me here, Wolf," argued Armand. "I can handle a gun."

Wolf snapped his fingers as if he had forgotten what the youth had done in the cave. "You sure can, boy! Okay, you stay. Girl! Get going!"

Jarrell and Diego pulled close to the wagon as Rosa placed Josefina on her horse and mounted up behind her. For a brief moment, Rosa's eyes locked with those of the marshal.

"I love you, Rosa," he said tenderly.

"And I love you, my Stuart," she said, smiling through her fear. Then wheeling the horse, she galloped away, leading Wolf's sorrel.

Wolf was readying the Gatling for action. Lifting his dark eyes and looking at Jarrell, he said in his low-pitched voice, "I thought so."

The marshal grinned at Wolf and looked back to see Rosa's long black hair flying in the wind as she rode toward the rock formation.

Wolf quickly told Armand and the two men to tie their horses to the harness of the wagon team. He wanted all the animals in one spot so he could swivel the Gatling in three directions.

"Get under the wagon!" he shouted. "You'll be harder to hit. Position yourselves so you can shoot in all three directions!"

Pulling rifles and ammunition from the wagon bed, Jarrell and the two Mexicans dived under the wagon.

The charging horde of fifteen Mexican guerrillas was now only four hundred yards away. Wolf released the safety catch that held the Gatling's crank. Hunkering down, he swung the ten deadly muzzles in the direction of the thundering Mexicans. Hollering to the men underneath the wagon, he said, "I'm going to cut loose first! You fellas follow up!"

He waited until the guerrillas were within two hundred yards. Then lining his gaze along the long tubular casing, he aimed into the center of the riders and turned the crank. The deep-throated rapid fire of the big machine gun spit instant death as several men and horses went down.

The remaining guerrillas immediately spread out to come at the wagon from two sides. From underneath it, guns were barking. Wolf swung the Gatling to catch the riders coming from his left, and when he fired, the big gun boomed in a staccato, dropping more men and horses in a hail of hot lead.

Bullets were plowing dirt around the wagon and chewing into its sides, showering Wolf and the other men with splinters.

Armand Tejada's only experience with firearms had been with pistols, and he was having trouble hitting anyone with the rifle he was using. Laying it aside, he picked up a .49 caliber Dragoon revolver from the pile of guns under the wagon. Earing back the hammer, he saw a guerrilla whose horse had just gone down with a bullet in its head.

The Mexican was on his feet less than fifty yards away. He bellied down and opened fire on the three men under the wagon. A bullet ripped through Stuart Jarrell's hat, barely missing his scalp.

Armand drew a bead on the guerrilla and fired. The slug bit dirt directly in front of the man, throwing dust in his eyes. Armand thumbed back the hammer again, and this time, allowing for the gun's tendency to shoot low, he sighted, lifted the muzzle slightly, and squeezed the trigger. When the gun bucked against his palm, the man slumped to the ground. Armand's bullet had gone through his left eye and out the back of his head.

Bodies of men and horses were strewn about the area. Seven guerrillas were dead.

The remaining eight were strung out, circling toward

the front of the wagon. For the moment, this put them in the neutral zone, where Wolf could not aim the machine gun.

Diego saw what they were doing. Grabbing two Navy Colt revolvers, he rolled out from under the left side of the wagon, and pointing a gun at the right side, shouted, "I am going to send them around that way, Señor Wolf!"

Suddenly, he leaped to his feet and ran toward the cluster of riders, both guns blazing. The guerrillas bolted their horses the opposite direction, but two of them peeled out of their saddles, cut down by Diego's bullets.

Five of the remaining six spread out to come from every direction. They were shouting to each other that they must get the man inside the wagon.

As they began the charge, guns spitting fire, one of the guerrillas veered off and headed at a full gallop toward the castle-shaped rock. Jarrell saw him and knew it meant one thing: He had seen Rosa's long hair flying when she had ridden for safety, and he figured he could hush the Gatling with a female hostage.

Quickly, Jarrell rolled out from under the wagon and dashed to his horse. Untying the reins from the harness, he vaulted into the saddle and spurred the animal for the big rock. He could hear the guttural roar of the Gatling behind him.

Setting his line of sight on the Mexican ahead of him, Jarrell knew the man would beat him to the rock by almost a minute. If Rosa and Josefina were anywhere in sight, the guerrilla would have time to get hold of one of them and put a gun to her head.

The marshal knew Rosa had her revolver, but he wondered if she would try to use it with little Josefina close by. In an exchange of gunfire, the child could get hit.

Jarrell watched as the Mexican leaped from his horse, gun drawn, and disappeared behind the rock. The marshal gouged his horse's sides, getting all the speed the animal could produce.

In just over half a minute, the horse skidded to a halt, and Jarrell jumped from the saddle while the horse was still in motion. Gun in hand, he flattened himself against the base of the huge rock and then eased his way toward where he had seen the Mexican disappear.

Coming around the blind side, he saw a wide cleavage in the rock's base. There were voices coming from high up. Muscles tense, the marshal made his way toward them. He could hear Rosa pleading with the man in Spanish.

Jarrell knew enough Spanish to understand that the guerrilla was demanding that she give him the child. Being small, Josefina would make the best hostage.

Easing out into the bright sunlight, the marshal saw the guerrilla looking up at Rosa, who was high on a ledge, holding the terrorized child.

Drawing a bead on where the Mexican's chest would be when he turned around, the marshal shouted, "Hey, you! Drop the gun!"

The swarthy-skinned guerrilla, startled, whirled around, bringing his gun with him. Jarrell's revolver roared, sending its missile of death into the man's heart. He collapsed in a heap, his legs bent under his body in a grotesque manner.

Rosa and Josefina climbed down into Jarrell's strong arms. He soothed the frightened little girl and then took Rosa in his arms and kissed her.

"Gracias." Rosa smiled up at him.

"For the kiss?"

"For the rescue," she said, pulling his head down. Kissing him soundly, she breathed, "Gracias, gracias. That is for the kisses!"

Five minutes after Stuart Jarrell had ridden away, the swiveling, thundering Gatling gun, along with Diego's and Armand's accurate shots, had dropped all the guerrillas but one. Realizing his dangerous predicament, this last man turned his horse and galloped away, but Wolf swung the gun toward him and turned the crank. Four rounds went off before hammers slammed on empty chambers.

One of the four slugs caught the fleeing Mexican's horse in the rump, and the animal went down with a scream, throwing its rider, who adeptly rolled to his feet. Quickly, the guerrilla spotted a riderless horse that had escaped the gunfire, standing about forty yards from him.

Wolf was about the same distance from the horse. He wanted to take the guerrilla alive if possible, so the man could tell him where the others were. Wolf wanted to steer clear of them.

Leaping out of the wagon, he ran toward the horse to head off the Mexican. With his long strides, he was gaining, when suddenly the horse became frightened and bolted away.

Wolf and the guerrilla were fifty feet apart when the Mexican pulled his revolver and fired. Being on the run, he missed by six feet, but he raised the gun again. Wolf closed in, drawing his right-hand Colt. "Don't try it!" he shouted.

The Mexican stopped and took aim.

Wolf's gun roared. He purposely winged the man, hitting him in the shoulder. The guerrilla's gun fell in the dirt, and Wolf stepped up and kicked it. Looking down at the man holding his bleeding shoulder, Wolf said, "I want to know where the rest of your army is. Was Aldo Vomero in this bunch we just killed?"

Giving Wolf a stubborn look, the guerrilla said, "I tell you nothing, dirty gringo." Rolling his tongue in his mouth, he spit in Wolf's face.

Rage flared in Wolf Bixler's black surly eyes.

The Mexican spit again, hissing, "I never tell you, devil gringo. Never!" He spit a third time.

Wolf's mouth framed a silent violent word, and he glared hotly at the Mexican, sleeving the spittle from his face.

Then the Mexican made a fatal mistake. From a scabbard on the back of his belt, he pulled a knife. With a roar that resembled that of a grizzly, Wolf Bixler batted the knife out of the guerrilla's hand and picked him up. The Mexican screamed as Wolf raised him over his head and then slammed him savagely to the ground.

Like a cat, Wolf came down, yanked the man to his knees, stepped behind him, and took hold of his head with both hands. Bones snapped and popped as he gave the man's head one violent wrench.

Dropping the dead man like a rag doll, Wolf straightened up. Mumbling to the lifeless form, he said, "I don't do that to somebody unless they make me mad. You made me mad."

Chapter Fifteen

Aldo Vomero stood over the twisted corpse of the guerrilla with the broken neck. Shaking his head, he lifted his eyes to the crumpled and sprawled bodies of men and horses spread over five acres of ground.

The bodies, dead a week now, were already beginning to decompose. A stench of rotting flesh tainted the crisp January air.

Fishing in his shirt pocket, Vomero pulled out the note he had found in the cave and read it again.

> Aldo,
>   I will be dead by the time you return. It was Tejada's man Bixler and those with him. They thought I was dead when they left. Took the Gatling. They are to meet a Dido Gomez at the Alamo in San Antonio. *Get them*.
>   Roberto

Aldo Vomero's blood surged. His savage face whipped around to the nine men who sat their horses behind him. Through clenched teeth he said with brittle words, "This Bixler and the others will pay! They will pay! Do you hear me? They will pay!"

With a malignant vengeance, the guerrilla leader rode north, his men following.

*   *   *

It was the first week of February when Wolf Bixler
and his group came down out of the Sierra Madres and
worked their way across the flat prairie toward the Rio
Grande River.

Bixler had not revealed to anyone his plan to give the
Gatling gun to the Comanches. His fellow travelers
knew only that they were safer with the gun along, and
they were glad to have it. Wolf kept the flaps closed on
both ends of the covered wagon, so as to conceal the
big machine gun from anyone who might come near.

Stuart Jarrell and Rosa Tejada had fallen deeper in
love, and Josefina was now calling the United States
marshal "Uncle Stu." Armand was pleased about the
romance. It would be fine with him if they ended up
married. Though Wolf was going back to prison at
Waco, Armand would live there so he could visit Wolf
every day. When the day came that his big friend was
released, they could live together for the rest of their
lives. He had shared these plans with no one as yet; he
would reveal them when the time was right.

Wolf had taken time in the evenings, after camp had
been set up, to teach Armand more about guns. He had
even shown the youth how to operate the Gatling and
had allowed him to fire off a few rounds, just to get the
feel of the big gun.

Rosa had mixed emotions about her brother's relationship with Wolf. Armand needed to know how to
handle weapons, but he was also taking on the hard
approach to life that he saw in his hero. She knew that
soon Wolf Bixler would be out of Armand's life, and she
comforted herself with that thought.

Rosa had Wolf figured out. He had gotten close to
Armand because their relationship was a man-to-man
situation, involving no tenderness, no sentimentality.
But in order to accept Josefina's love and affection,
Wolf would have to give up his stern manner. However, Rosa told herself, God had made females the
subtle ones. They could undermine a man's defenses

without him knowing it. If anyone could ever make Wolf smile, Rosa knew it would be little Josefina.

Late in the afternoon on February 10, 1877, the travelers saw the Rio Grande River come into view. On the Mexican side stood the town of Nuevo Laredo, and just across it was Laredo, Texas.

Stuart Jarrell pulled his horse alongside the rumbling covered wagon so that he and Wolf could discuss the problem of getting the wagon across the river. They dared not take it over the bridge into Laredo since the United States authorities there were sure to confiscate the Gatling.

Jarrell mentioned the possibility of leaving the wagon and machine gun behind, but corrected himself immediately, saying that it was one hundred fifty miles to San Antonio. Aldo Vomero's guerrillas could show up at any time. Even if Aldo had been one of the guerrillas they had killed, the others would want the Gatling back. They would also want vengeance for their compadres who had been wiped out. The covered wagon would not be difficult to trail, and so the travelers needed to keep the Gatling with them.

Wolf did not say a thing when Jarrell spoke at first of leaving the wagon and Gatling gun behind. There was no way he was going to give up the machine gun. He was determined to put it into Iron Face's hands.

The decision was made to go a few miles upstream and camp in the woods. There they would build a raft and float the wagon across the river at night. They would use the axes in the wagon to cut down enough trees to form the raft, and the rope would serve to tie the logs together.

The travelers parked the covered wagon in a small clearing among the trees in the dense forest, some fifty yards from the west bank of the Rio Grande River. Working in the dappled sunlight that filtered through the towering pines, Wolf, Jarrell, and Diego chopped trees. Wolf had assigned Armand Tejada to stand at the west side of the clearing and look beyond the forest to the open land. If Vomero's guerrillas were trailing them, they would be coming from that direction.

While the sound of the axes biting into wood rang through the trees, Josefina Montoya whispered to Rosa that she had to go relieve herself.

"All right," responded Rosa. "I will take you over there into the woods."

"I am old enough to go by myself," the child said, feeling a growing independence.

Smiling at her niece, Rosa said, "Do not go too far." Pointing northwest, she added, "Go that way."

Josefina sent a friendly wave to Armand as she angled away from him and disappeared into the deep-shaded thicket.

Earlier that same day, five men had ridden up to the Pecos bank in Laredo, Texas, and dismounted. B. J. Barton and his gang were wanted by the law all over south Texas for bank robbery. They were about to give the authorities one more reason to want them.

Barton's four cohorts were Lester Garrelson, Frank Comstock, Marley Kemper, and Jess Nichols.

Moments later, the Barton gang came out of the bank, bearing full money sacks, guns blazing. Riding hard, they headed north along the east bank of the Rio Grande. Their plan was to cross into Mexico upriver at a heavily wooded area.

As B. J. Barton and his gang rode their horses through the belly-deep water of the river, they could hear chopping sounds coming from deeper in the woods. Sliding from their saddles as they drew up on the bank, they tied the animals in the shade and pulled their guns.

Creeping closer in the mottled sunlight, the five outlaws saw three men swinging axes. Lester Garrelson said, "Boss, there's a Mexican kid standin' off to the west. Seems to be watchin' for somebody."

But B. J. Barton's gaze had fallen on the shapely Mexican woman who stood near the covered wagon.

"I wonder what's in the wagon," spoke up Marley Kemper.

"Looks like we're about to find out." Jess Nichols chuckled.

"I want what's *outside* the wagon," breathed Barton. "Let's go."

Wolf Bixler and Stuart Jarrell were carrying a log to the spot where they had framed up the raft, when suddenly Barton, Garrelson, Comstock, and Nichols leaped from the dense thicket. "Hold it right there!" bellowed Barton.

Wolf's head snapped up, and Jarrell saw instantly that the gunmen had the drop on them.

Nichols put cold eyes on Diego Corral, who stood over a fallen tree, ax in hand. "Put the ax down, greaser," he said, training his gun on Diego's chest.

Diego let the ax drop and lean against the tree that lay at his feet, the handle slightly elevated.

Jess Nichols was disarming Rosa, Diego, Wolf, and Jarrell when Marley Kemper appeared, pushing Armand in front of him. Armand's revolver was in Kemper's left hand.

His lustful eyes on Rosa, Barton said from the side of his mouth, "Frank, look in the wagon. See what's in there."

Nichols laid the five revolvers on a waist-high tree stump and then stood beside the stump, sneering.

Stuart Jarrell bristled as B. J. Barton moved close to Rosa. She looked at the outlaw leader with cold contempt.

"You're goin' with me, honey baby," Barton said, smiling wickedly.

When Jarrell took a step toward Barton, Jess Nichols barked, "Hold it, cowboy!"

Jarrell checked his move, looking down the black muzzle of Nichols's gun.

Frank Comstock turned from the wagon carrying a man's coat with a badge pinned to its front. "We got a Gatling gun in the wagon, boss," he said. "New ten-barrel kind. Several rifles and pistols. Ammunition, too, and some rope." Holding the coat, badge forward, he added levelly, "One of these dudes is a U.S. marshal."

Barton's trenchant eyes skipped from man to man. "Couldn't be the kid or the skinny greaser," he said. "Bearded guy is too big for the coat. Has to be Long John, here, who seems to be honey baby's boyfriend."

Stuart Jarrell's angular jaw jutted. "I'm a U.S. marshal, all right," he said with grit in his voice. "You'd best back out of whatever you had in mind and clear out of here."

Insolence rippled Barton's heavy jowls. He was a thick-bodied man, with sloping, bull-like shoulders. "Well, you ain't in the U.S. at the moment, Marshal," he sneered. "Even if it was you with the gun in your hand, and me at your mercy, you couldn't arrest me. I'm standin' on Mexican soil."

"You don't know what you're talking about, mister," growled Jarrell.

"Ain't you heard, Marshal? Tejada ain't president of Mexico no more. Mister Díaz is. Ain't no extradition pact now."

"You're wrong," Jarrell snapped. "We've talked to people all across Mexico. Díaz hasn't been installed yet as president. Won't be for some time. Tejada's agreement stands until the Mexican government officially revokes it. An American lawman can come into Mexico and arrest anybody who has committed a crime in the States."

Marley Kemper spoke up, his voice filled with worry. "Boss, you said we'd be safe if we crossed the border. Now what are we gonna—"

"Shut up!" Barton lashed. "We're gonna take their guns and what money they got and hightail it outta here." Slipping an arm around Rosa's waist, he said, "And honey baby is comin' with me."

Rosa jerked herself free of his grasp, anger flaring in her ebony eyes. Barton laughed. "Hey! I like a woman with some fire!"

"Keep your filthy hands off her!" Jarrell shouted, his voice cutting the air like a clap of thunder.

The outlaw's head whipped around. "What are you gonna do about it, Marshal?"

"*I'll break your filthy neck!*" Jarrell barked, the tidal wave within him moving toward a violent crest.

"With a bullet in your gut?" sneered Barton.

Stuart Jarrell knew if the gang took Rosa, he would never see her again. When the outlaw leader was through with her, he would kill her. There was only one chance for her; he would have to kill the man—and there was only one way he could do it.

"Hey, you!" roared Jarrell, hot savagery in his eyes.

"My name's Barton, Marshal," the outlaw said. "B. J. Barton. Be more respectful."

With a smirk on his face, Jarrell said challengingly, "You're a yellow-livered, scaly-bellied coward!"

A smoldering rage surfaced on Barton's cheeks. He set a pair of murderous eyes on the tall man.

"You're tough stuff with your friends standing here holding a gun on me," rasped Jarrell. "If it was just you and me, you'd slither back under your rock with your yellow stripe showing."

There was a silent pause. B. J. Barton's men turned their eyes on him. The outlaw leader had never been confronted this way before.

Marley Kemper spoke up. "What you waitin' for, boss? You outweigh him by sixty or seventy pounds."

"I'm thinkin'," Barton grumbled. "Decidin' whether to just beat him up good, or kill him."

"If you're man enough to fight me, Barton," said Jarrell, "it'll be with knives. To the death."

B. J. Barton was in a spot. He would lose his leadership with these men if he did not accept the challenge. Taking a deep breath and swelling up his huge chest, he said hotly, "You got it."

Rosa looked on with horror as the two men stripped to the waist despite the nip in the air. It would be Barton's bulk against Jarrell's lean, sinewy, hard frame.

On Frank Comstock's waist hung a large knife, which he handed to Barton. The outlaw boss told his men not to interfere, no matter what happened. He was going to kill this cocky marshal and ride away with the wench.

Wolf Bixler offered Jarrell his knife, and when the marshal stepped close to take it from him, Wolf said, "Good luck, Stu."

"It'd be better for you if I had bad luck," he grinned. "Then you wouldn't have to go back to prison. You gave your word to *me*, not the U.S. government."

Fixing Jarrell with steady eyes, Wolf said, "Good luck, Stu."

As the two men met in the middle of the clearing, Barton grinned, a dry hunger in his eyes. "I'm gonna cut you to ribbons, tin badge," he said coldly.

The outlaw charged, swinging the deadly blade in a full arc, trying to open Jarrell's midsection, but the marshal leaped back out of range and popped Barton on the ear with his free fist. The blow stung, and with his ear ringing Barton came again, but missed with the blade a second time.

The men bobbed, weaved, clinched, separated, and circled, each trying to find an opening.

Jarrell's traveling companions stood breathlessly watching while Barton's men held them at gunpoint. Fearful for Jarrell's life, Rosa had completely forgotten about little Josefina, who was still out in the woods.

The child had become occupied with a wobbly porcupine. After watching the prickly animal for a while, she decided it was time to get back to the adults.

Upon approaching the clearing, Josefina saw the two men fighting and the outlaws holding guns on the others. She had seen enough of this kind of thing in past weeks to know that her people were in serious trouble. She noticed Wolf's Colts and the other revolvers lying on the tree stump. Jess Nichols was standing next to the stump, but his attention was on the knife fight.

From the shadows, Josefina studied the situation. The stump was about forty feet from where she stood, and Nichols's back was toward her. Wolf was some thirty feet past the stump, and Josefina was confident that if she could get a gun to Wolf, he could handle the bad men. She would have to sneak her way to the stump, pick up the gun, and run to Wolf with it as fast as she could go.

Taking a deep breath, she moved out of the shadows, creeping up behind Nichols. She knew that if she got caught, the bad men would hurt her . . . maybe kill her. A ball of ice formed in the pit of her stomach, the fear making her breath come in short gasps.

Taking each step carefully, she wiped her sweaty

palms on her dress so that her hands would be dry. Once she had hold of Wolf's gun, she did not want to drop it. She could feel a throbbing in her temples.

Wolf caught sight of Josefina at the same time Rosa did. Both of them immediately understood what she was doing.

Stuart Jarrell and B. J. Barton were on the ground in a cloud of dust, the outlaw on top of the marshal, attempting to drive his knife into Jarrell's chest. They were deadlocked, with Jarrell gripping Barton's quivering wrist, meeting it strength for strength.

Both Rosa and Wolf were watching the two men, but keeping Josefina in the periphery of their vision. Diego Corral had also caught sight of the little girl, who was almost to the stump. He eyed the ax handle that was only inches from his right hand.

As Josefina reached her trembling hand toward the Colt that was closest to the stump's edge, Jess Nichols shouted something to B. J. Barton, who had just been flipped off Jarrell, head over heels. The sudden shout startled the little girl, and she jerked her hand back, looking up at the outlaw, eyes bulging with fright. Nichols shifted his feet slightly but still did not see Josefina. He was intent on the fight. The two combatants were now facing each other, on their feet, puffing, moving slowly in circular fashion, knife blades gleaming in the sun.

Abruptly, Josefina seized Wolf's .45 caliber revolver by the barrel and darted toward him. She wanted to thrust the gun into his hand so all he had to do was cock it and fire.

As the frightened child ran toward Wolf, she had her eyes on him and did not see the small broken tree limbs that had been trimmed off the logs for the raft. Her feet tangled in the limbs, and she stumbled and fell, dropping the gun in front of her. It hit the ground six feet in front of Bixler.

Jess Nichols saw movement from the corner of his eye and turned his gaze from the fighting men to the little girl falling in the broken limbs. He caught sight of the Colt as it hit the ground and of Wolf diving for it.

Garrelson, Comstock, and Kemper were still intent on the fight, unaware of the commotion behind them. It wasn't until Diego, seeing Nichols bring his gun around on Wolf, grasped the ax and threw it at him, blade first, that they realized something was going on. With a sickening sodden sound, the sharp blade buried itself in the side of Nichols's head.

Wolf was in a prone position on the ground, ready to fire, but Josefina was right in front of him. Raising up on one knee to shoot over her, he fired at Comstock, who was bringing his gun around. The outlaw dropped like a lightning-struck tree.

Garrelson and Kemper saw Wolf's smoking muzzle, and realized they could never bring their weapons into play. It would be suicide to try.

"Throw down the guns!" roared Wolf, aiming his Colt.

Both men dropped their revolvers as if they had suddenly turned red-hot, and Armand was on hand to pick them up.

Rosa ran to Josefina, trying to watch the fight at the same time. Josefina had skinned her arms and knees on the rough bark of the broken limbs.

Jarrell had kicked the knife from Barton's hand and now had him flat on his back with the point of Wolf's knife at his sweaty throat. In cold terror, the outlaw was begging Jarrell not to kill him.

At that instant eight riders came thundering into the clearing, two of them wearing badges. As they halted in a cloud of dust, they saw B. J. Barton's predicament.

"Don't kill, him, mister!" cried out the older of the two lawmen.

Jarrell, who did not intend to kill Barton, looked up and puffed, "I'm United States marshal Stuart Jarrell. Who are you?"

"Name's Sam Pickford," came the reply. "I'm marshal of Laredo." Pointing at the man wearing a badge beside him, he said, "This is my son, Jed, my deputy. These other gentlemen are my posse. Barton's gang held up our bank this morning. Killed two people. We're taking them back to hang."

Diego was standing by the corpses of Jess Nichols and Frank Comstock. "These two will not kick much when you hang them, Señor Marshal," he said, showing his snow-white teeth.

When Pickford saw the ax blade buried in Nichols's head, he turned an ashen color.

Jarrell let Barton, quivering, stand up. "You can have him, Pickford. Wouldn't want to cheat the hangman."

Josefina remained with Armand while Rosa ran and embraced Jarrell, telling him tearfully that she loved him.

Marshal Sam Pickford thanked the travelers for subduing the bank robbers. Eyeing the Gatling in the covered wagon and the partially made raft, he asked what they were doing.

Stuart Jarrell explained the situation, introducing El Presidente Tejada's children and granddaughter to Pickford.

Laredo's marshal grinned and said, "We didn't find a thing out here in these woods except some good people these bank robbers were trying to molest."

The travelers watched the posse take the gang away, with Nichols and Comstock draped over their saddles.

Attention was immediately turned to the pretty little girl. Everyone except Wolf hugged Josefina, praising her courage and clear thinking in a time of great danger. When they were finished, Wolf came to her and laid his hand on top of her head. "That was good goin', little black-eyed girl," he said. "I'm very proud of you."

Smiling up at the towering man, Josefina replied, "Gracias, Uncle Wolf. I love you."

He stood there a few seconds, looking as though he wanted to say something to the child, but then just patted her head and walked away.

Josefina turned to Rosa, who was standing near her, and asked, "Why doesn't Uncle Wolf ever smile?"

Making sure the big man was out of earshot, Rosa said, "Uncle Wolf has had much unhappiness in his life, Josefina. You just keep calling him your uncle and keep telling him you love him. One of these days he will smile."

Chapter Sixteen

The days passed all too quickly for Rosa Tejada. She was fighting mixed emotions. She was eager to arrive in San Antonio and enjoy the safety that would be provided by Dido Gomez; it would also be a relief to be through with the wearisome travel. But a cloud of sadness overshadowed her thoughts of ending the journey. She would have to say good-bye to the man whom she had come to love so much.

On the night of February 20, they were camped alongside a small stream forty miles southwest of San Antonio. Everyone agreed that when they pulled out the next day, they would push on to San Antonio without stopping. The land was flat, so the going was relatively easy, and Wolf figured they would arrive at the Alamo before dawn on the twenty-third.

Rosa tucked Josefina in, kissed her good night, and watched the others slipping into their blankets. Since crossing the Rio Grande, the men had taken shifts at night keeping watch. There were no forests to hide in on the Texas plains.

First watch tonight belonged to Stuart Jarrell. He was sitting on a grassy mound near the bubbling stream. A half-moon in the sky kept ducking behind drifting clouds, and the stars winked silently.

As Rosa drew near to Jarrell, the tall marshal laid down his rifle and stood to meet her. He folded her into his arms, holding her close for a moment, and then looked down into her beautiful face. The stars seemed to desert the heavens and rush to nestle in her big dark eyes.

"I love you, Rosa," he said softly.

"I love you, too," she breathed, clinging to him, her head against his chest.

"Hey," he said, drawing back and looking into her eyes glistening with tears. "What's the matter, darling?"

"Oh, Stu," she said sadly, "we will be in San Antonio in less than two days. When will I ever see you again?"

Placing his hands on her cheeks, he smoothed out the tears that were falling. "I will have to go to Austin after I see you safely to Dido Gomez," he explained. "I'll be there for a few days, and then I'll go on to Waco to meet Wolf so I can escort him to the prison. When that's done, I'll be on another assignment. But just as soon as I can, I will come back to you."

"That sounds like a long time," Rosa said, blinking back her tears.

He was quiet for a moment, looking into her deep eyes. In his solitary moments over the past few weeks, he had thought of asking Rosa to become his wife, but his recent disappointment with Peggy Garner made him apprehensive.

His thoughts went back to the last time he had seen Peggy. The words he had spoken echoed through his mind. *If you really love me, you'll marry me no matter what I do for a living.*

Placing a fingertip under Rosa's graceful chin, he lowered his face and kissed her tenderly. Still clinging tightly to him, she tilted her head downward, laying her forehead against his chest.

Jarrell figured it was now or never. "Rosa . . ."

Keeping her forehead where it was, she whispered, "Yes?"

"Do you really love me the way you have said since that first night beside the canyon?"

Still holding her position, she answered, "More than ever since you risked your life to keep that Barton beast from taking me."

With his heart pounding, he asked, "If . . . if a woman

really loves a man, do you believe she would marry him no matter what he does for a living?"

"Of course," she said.

"Even if he was a lawman?"

Rosa pulled her head back. He watched her eyes lift to his. With a shaky voice she said, "Stu, what are you saying?"

"I'm not saying, Rosa. I'm asking."

"You . . . you are asking me to be your wife?"

"Yes."

Rosa's brow furrowed, and she lowered her eyes. "Oh, Stu, I—"

"Rosa, I realize we've known each other only a short time, but who's to say how long it takes to fall in love? I know in Mexico lengthy courtships are the custom, but—"

"Oh, no, Stu, it's not that," she interrupted. "Not at all. I have no doubts that what you and I feel for each other is real and will last. I want to say yes. I want to very much. I want to become your wife, to live my life with you, but . . . but—"

"Is it the badge, then?"

Raising her eyes back to his, she lifted a hand and stroked his cheek. "No, my darling. I love the man behind the badge, and I would be proud to be the wife of a United States marshal."

"Then what is it, Rosa?" he asked.

"I have a responsibility to Armand and Josefina. I may never see my father again. If not, I must finish raising Armand, and I will have Josefina, whatever happens. She has no one else."

The tall man's face broke into a broad grin. "Is *that* what's bothering you?"

"Yes. I cannot ask you to take a wife and a niece and brother, too!"

He laughed loudly. "You don't have to ask me to take Armand and Josefina into our home. I am volunteering! Now. Will you marry me?"

Tears again spilled on Rosa's cheeks. "Oh, yes, my love. *Yes!*"

The pale moonlight cast a silver veil around them.

Rosa's tenderness and beauty warmed the chilly night air, stirring his masculine senses. He pressed her close to him and kissed her fervently.

With the coming of dawn, the happy young couple announced their engagement to the group. Josefina was thrilled, and Armand and Diego offered their congratulations. Wolf said he had seen it coming. Jarrell informed them that a date would be set after they arrived in San Antonio and learned what living arrangements Gomez had made for Rosa, Josefina, and Armand. It would take some time for Jarrell to ready things at his house in Waco.

The weary travelers pulled into San Antonio at four in the morning on February 23, 1877, an hour before dawn.

Rosa sat next to Wolf on the wagon seat, holding a sleeping Josefina. The wagon wheels squeaked as the procession moved past darkened adobe houses on Patrero Street. There was no sign of life.

Suddenly a big dog came out from under a porch, barking ferociously. Josefina jerked awake at the noise. The dog chased them half a block and then returned to its lair.

They turned onto Travis Street, and moments later the dark, hulking outline of the Alamo's chapel loomed above them, outlined against the starlit Texas sky.

"Is this where we are going to stay?" asked Josefina, rubbing sleepy eyes.

"For a little while," Rosa told her.

Armand squinted against the gloom, trying to see the ponderous mission more clearly. Some of the walls and buildings had been rebuilt, but rubble was still strewn about in places. *So this is where it happened,* he thought. *This is where history was made amid roaring cannons, barking rifles, fire, smoke, and the mingled blood of the Mexicans and Texans.*

The place seemed so quiet and peaceful in that hour before dawn.

Stuart Jarrell swung from his saddle and opened the squeaky iron gate, and the procession moved through. Drawing up in front of the battle-and-weather-pitted chapel, the travelers lowered themselves from wagon and horses to the ground and then huddled at the huge front door.

Wolf tapped on the solid oak door and waited. When there was no response, he knocked again, harder. Within seconds there was a shuffling sound, followed by the clatter of metal. Groaning on its one-hundred-fifty-year-old hinges, the door swung open, allowing the yellow light of a lantern to escape into the predawn darkness.

A swarthy Mexican man with a thick mop of black hair hoisted the lantern close to the big man's face. "Who are you?" he asked.

"Wolf Bixler," came the deep-voiced reply. "Dido Gomez?"

"Sí," he said, swinging the door wider. "Come in."

As the travelers entered, Gomez closed the door. There were five rooms off the nave, two on each side and one in the rear. The rooms on each side were not adjacent, however, since twelve feet of wall stretched between them, giving the chapel an irregular shape. From the outside, the rooms formed alcoves into which no one could see.

"You have made it safely," Gomez sighed, holding the lantern so as to study their faces. "This must be Armand, and the beautiful one must be Rosa. Who is the little one?"

"She is our niece, Josefina Montoya," Rosa explained. "Her parents were killed along with my mother. My father decided to send her with us after he had sent the message to you."

"And these gentlemen?"

"This is Diego Corral—" said Rosa.

"Ah, your guide," Gomez interrupted.

"No," Rosa responded flatly. "Our guide was killed. We will tell you about it later. Diego came along to help care for Josefina." Laying a hand on the marshal's arm, she said, "This is United States marshal Stuart Jarrell. He was not a planned member of the traveling party, but it worked out this way."

"Well," said Dido Gomez, "you all look to be very

tired. Let us get you bedded down so you can get some sleep before the sun comes up."

Gomez showed them an open stable near the boarded-up barracks, and the horses were placed behind a double-rail fence. The covered wagon was pulled up in an alcove of the chapel on the side facing the convent, and bedrolls were carried into the chapel through a side door near where the wagon was parked.

Inside the chapel, Gomez set the lantern on a dusty table in the high-ceilinged nave. Suggesting that they might wish to sleep privately, he pointed out several rooms where they could bed down.

Stuart Jarrell stood gazing around the cold stone walls in the light of the lantern. He thought of the bloody battle that had taken place there some forty-one years ago. Suddenly Gomez's voice seemed remote and infinitesimal, and Jarrell seemed to hear the sound of guns booming, men shouting, and harried footsteps clattering across the stone floor of the nave.

Slowly, the sounds of battle faded away, and Jarrell blinked and ran his gaze around the shadowy walls again. A cold chill ran through his body. The austere building seemed haunted by the ghosts of Jim Bowie, Daniel Cloud, Davy Crockett, and a hundred seventy-nine other valiant men who had eaten their last meal, seen their last sunset, and breathed their last breath in the Alamo. The three acres of land within the rectangular walls of the old Franciscan mission were hallowed ground to Stuart Jarrell.

His thoughts were pulled back to the present as Rosa kissed his cheek and led Josefina to a room a few feet away. "Oh . . . uh, good night," he responded as she smiled at him and closed the door.

Dido Gomez noticed Diego Corral studying him closely as he described the different rooms available. He felt uncomfortable under the pressure of the thin man's gaze.

Pointing across the nave to the far door, Gomez said, "Señor Jarrell, may I suggest that you and Armand take that room. That is the baptistery."

Jarrell and Armand carried their bedrolls to the designated room.

Gesturing toward a door on the opposite side of the nave, Gomez said, "Señor Bixler, you are a large man. I think you would be most comfortable in that room over there."

Wolf was eager to discuss the gold with Tejada's man, and so looking down at him, he said, "Before I turn in, Gomez, I need to talk to you privately for just a moment. Go ahead and get Diego settled."

Nodding in assent, Gomez pointed out another room. "In that room there is a small cot that is just your size, Señor Corral."

His bedroll in his arms, Diego walked toward the room.

"Oh, Señor Corral," Gomez spoke up suddenly. "I should go with you. There are some things you may stumble over if I do not guide you." Turning to Wolf, he whispered, "I believe that he and I know each other from someplace. I think I know where, but I must ask him. It is quite personal. I will be back in a moment."

Wolf nodded and watched Gomez and Diego enter the room, the door clicking shut behind them.

Faint moonlight was shining through a dirty window as the two men stepped into the dark room. Pushing the door shut, Gomez said in a low voice, "Actually, Señor Corral, I wanted to ask you a private question."

"Oh?"

"Sí. You seem to be examining me quite closely. We have met before, perhaps?"

Peering at the other man in the obscure light of the moon, Diego said, "That is for you to say, señor. I had dinner once in El Presidente Tejada's mansion with several of his associates. Dido Gomez was there. It has been some time, of course, but I am trying to remember. I do not think Dido Gomez looked like you."

Five seconds passed before the other man spoke. In a cold, level tone, he said, "Domingo."

Suddenly, a huge man emerged from the shadows and seized Diego from behind, clamping a hand over his mouth.

Diego's eyes bulged as Gomez said, "The others will be here by sunrise, Domingo. Maybe before. We will wait to kill the rest when we are more in number. This one must die now. He knows."

Diego struggled, hoping to make a noise of some kind that would bring Wolf Bixler, but Domingo's strength was too much. Diego could not budge.

"Dido Gomez is dead, Señor Corral," the imposter said, in a tone suggesting that he was gloating over this fact. "We killed him for our friend Porfirio Díaz—and for a nice fee, also, you understand. I am Enrico Kaleta."

Diego's eyes bulged even more.

"You know my name, I see." The man grinned evilly. "Then you also know Domingo Herrera, the man who is about to kill you!"

Diego knew that Enrico Kaleta and Domingo Herrera were Mexico's two most infamous hired killers. Díaz, taking no chances, had a back-up plan in case the trap set by Pedro Llamas and Aldo Vomero failed. Rosa, Armand, and Josefina were to die, even if Díaz did not get to handle it personally, and Kaleta and Herrera certainly would not fail.

Diego's breath was coming in short, wheezing gasps. He was going to die at the hands of Domingo Herrera.

"We are the ones who killed Tejada's wife and daughter in Mexico City," boasted Kaleta. "His son-in-law, too. We shot the pig Tejada himself, but his body-guards kept us from killing him. While he hides out, we will kill his other children and his granddaughter, too. One day Tejada will show up somewhere, and we will get him. Your big friend Bixler will die because he killed the Salazar brothers. Too bad you have to die, Señor Corral. You were just along for the ride."

Diego tried again, but he could not break Domingo's hold.

Kaleta moved to the door. "Watch for our comrades, Domingo," he said. "They know to come past the window, as always, so you can identify them. If any of these people are awake at that time, I will say that Abrelio, Eloy, Felipe, and Arturo are friends of El President Tejada. Kill this one now. Viva Díaz!"

Kaleta stepped out of the room, closing the heavy door behind him. Just before it clicked shut, Diego made a last, futile attempt to free himself from Domingo Herrera's grasp. As Diego struggled, Domingo slipped a knife from a sheath on his belt and plunged it into Diego's back, the blade puncturing the right lung.

Keeping his hand over the thin man's mouth, the killer pulled the knife out and then brutally plunged it in again. This time the blade went lower, lancing through a kidney, and Diego slumped to the floor, somehow not yet losing consciousness. He was dying and he knew it as he lay there bleeding profusely.

Considering the thin man dead—though he could not see him in the deep shadows on the floor—Domingo wiped the blood from the knife and dropped it back into its sheath. Lifting one foot onto a stool, he peered out the window. It would be dawn soon, and his cohorts would be returning.

From his position on the floor behind Herrera, Diego breathed through his mouth, making no sound. There was one thing he had to do before he died—the others had to be warned.

He could see in the moonlight the knife handle protruding from the sheath on Herrera's belt. Pain racked his body and blood was coming from his mouth.

He felt an almost overwhelming desire to cough but suppressed it. Holding his breath, he silently pulled himself to his feet, using the wall for support. Dizziness washed over him as he swayed for a few seconds, but then it passed. He would get only one chance, and he must not fail.

Summoning his strength, he carefully lifted the knife out of the sheath. Grasping the handle with both hands, he raised the knife. In the same instant, the killer suddenly turned, looking him in the eyes. Diego brought the knife down savagely, driving the blade into Domingo Herrera's heart.

Herrera dropped in a heap, his hands clutching the handle of the knife. Diego staggered toward the door.

In the nave, Wolf Bixler turned from the imposter Kaleta, who had assured him that he would have his gold the next day, and picked up his bedroll. "See you in a couple of hours, Gomez," he said, yawning.

Hearing the door of Diego's room squeak on its hinges, Wolf glanced in that direction and saw Diego stagger into the light, blood running from his mouth.

Enrico Kaleta tensed.

"This man . . . is . . . not Gomez," Diego gasped.

From the corner of his eye, Wolf saw Kaleta go for his gun. He slung the bedroll in Kaleta's face, throwing him off balance, and with lightning speed he drew both Colt .45s and fired. Kaleta's gun discharged, and a bullet ricocheted off the stone floor and buried itself in a wooden door casing. The killer fell flat on his back, his sightless eyes staring toward the lofty ceiling.

Doors were opening as Wolf dashed to Diego, who had slumped to the floor. Picking him up carefully, Wolf carried the dying man to the small table that held the lantern and placed him on the floor beside it.

Jarrell, Armand, and Rosa—each with a gun in hand—gathered around as Wolf knelt beside Diego. Gun smoke hung in the still air like a fog. Rosa whimpered as her eyes fell on Diego.

Looking up at the marshal, Wolf said, "Stu, check every room in this place." Pointing to the open door from where Diego had emerged, he added, "Startin' with that one over there. If there's anybody else hidin' around here, I want to know it. But be careful."

Jarrell picked up a nearby lantern and lit it. Gun ready, he began his search. Armand gave Diego a fond look and went with the marshal.

Rosa knelt beside Wolf, looking down at the dying man. There was bloody spittle collecting at the corners of his mouth, and the flame of the lantern reflected off the sweaty sheen on his skin.

"Oh, Diego," whispered Rosa, her voice trembling.

The thin Mexican looked up dully at Wolf. "Man . . . man you shot is En . . . Enrico Kaleta."

Wolf and Rosa looked at each other. They both knew the name.

Diego coughed. "Man who stabbed me . . . is Domingo . . . Herrera. They . . . they . . ."

"Do not try to talk, Diego," Rosa said tenderly.

Wolf had lifted his eyes toward the room where Diego was stabbed when Jarrell appeared. "Dead man in here, Wolf. Looks like Diego killed him."

Wolf nodded. Jarrell and Armand continued their search.

Diego coughed again. "I . . . must tell you," he murmured to Wolf, willing himself alive. "They . . . killed El Presidente's wife and the others. More . . . more of Díaz's men will be here . . . sunrise."

At that moment Rosa felt Josefina come up beside her. The sleepy-eyed child looked down compassionately at the bleeding man.

Diego lifted a hand and clutched Wolf's shirt sleeve. "Do not let them hurt . . . the children . . . señor," he pleaded.

"I won't," Wolf replied.

The little man coughed once more and was gone.

Tears brimmed Rosa's eyes, and when Josefina realized Diego was dead, she too began to sob.

Wolf stood and said to Rosa, "Find something to cover him. I don't know how many of Díaz's men are comin', but I'm bringin' the Gatling gun inside."

Chapter Seventeen

As dawn came to the windswept Texas plains, Aldo Vomero and his nine men rode into San Antonio from the southwest, the cold wind nipping at their faces.

At the same moment, Enrico Kaleta's friends were approaching from due east. They passed through an area thick with adobe houses and saw lights beginning to flicker in some of the opaque windows. As they drew up to the big iron gate of the Alamo, the one called Felipe dismounted and swung it open.

Suddenly the sound of many hooves on the hard-packed street met the ears of the four men at the gate. They turned and saw ten men on horseback round the corner less than a block away. They had no idea who the riders were, but they did not wish to be seen entering the Alamo.

"Hurry!" said Felipe in a hushed voice. "Get inside so I can close the gate!"

One of Aldo Vomero's men pointed toward the four figures and said, "Aldo! Look!"

Vomero's riders spurred their horses to a gallop, closing in fast. As they reached the gate, Felipe, Abrelio, Eloy, and Arturo were dashing for the chapel, but in their haste they had left the gate open.

Vomero spotted the covered wagon beside the chapel and assumed the four men were part of the bunch that had stolen the Gatling gun. His voice barbed with rage, he shouted, "Kill them!"

A volley of gunfire exploded, violently disrupting San Antonio's dawn repose. The four fleeing Mexicans fell dead under the hail of hot lead.

Inside the chapel, Wolf Bixler and the others were discussing their plan of defense against the unknown number of Enrico Kaleta's men that Diego had said were coming. Wolf had brought in the Gatling gun and all the other weapons from the covered wagon, along with the ammunition. When the chapel doors were bolted, the big machine gun was placed on the floor with its ten deadly muzzles trained on the main door.

Wolf had ripped loose the bolts that held the Gatling's base to the wagon bed, and so the rapid-fire weapon now rested intact and complete on its base, ready for action.

Rosa had covered Diego's lifeless form and put Josefina back to bed. Wolf had dragged Kaleta's body into the vestibule, placing it out of sight.

Stuart Jarrell reported to Wolf that the rooms of the chapel were all empty except the one that held Domingo Herrera's body. He pointed out that each corner room had two windows from which they could shoot if necessary.

At that moment the gunfire erupted in the Alamo's courtyard.

Wolf, Jarrell, and Armand dashed to the corner room nearest the noise and peered through the dusty window. They saw the band of riders with smoking guns move through the gate, and they saw four dead men on the ground. One of Vomero's men was headed for the covered wagon.

Jarrell looked at Wolf, puzzled, and said, "What do you suppose is going on?"

"I have no idea," he responded, "but the big bunch sure didn't like the little bunch."

Their bewilderment was short-lived. They understood exactly what had happened when a heavy voice with a strong Spanish accent came from the courtyard. "You inside the chapel! Bixler! I am Aldo Vomero! We have just exterminated four of your compadres. I am a man of little patience. My men and I have come all the way from Mexico. I want my Gatling gun back! I know you have it in there, so let us not play games."

Jarrell said, "Wolf, I count ten men. The way I see it, they want more than the Gatling."

"Yeah," nodded the big man, making his own count. "They are after your gal and the two kids. You're right, there's ten. We've got to fight them. No other choice."

They returned to the nave, and quickly the decision was made that one person would occupy each of the four corner rooms and shoot from the windows. With rifles and pistols, they would try to hold off Vomero's band. Wolf said that if eventually they attempted to come through either of the doors, he would dash to the Gatling and use it on them.

Rosa and Armand would take the corner rooms on the far side of the chapel, and Jarrell and Wolf would take the rooms on the convent side, where the Mexican guerrillas now stood. Josefina, who had joined them, saying she couldn't sleep, was told that she would take cover in the baptistery room at the back, where she would be safe.

Standing near the side door by the covered wagon, Aldo Vomero shouted, "Bixler! I am giving you a chance! Throw down your guns and come out! I promise no one will be harmed. I only want my Gatling gun!"

"He's lying," Jarrell said to Wolf, putting an arm around Rosa. "Armand, Josefina, and Rosa here are already marked for death. Vomero isn't going to let you and me walk away."

"Like I said," Wolf repeated, "we've got no choice. We have to fight them."

Wolf had accepted the fact that there would be no gold for the Comanches, but at least he would do his best to get the Gatling into their hands.

"You have five minutes!" boomed Vomero's voice. "Surrender, or you will die!"

Josefina stepped close to the big man, lifting her black, fearful eyes to him. "Uncle Wolf," she said with a quiver in her voice, "please do not let the bad men hurt us."

The bearded man looked down on her with a tenderness in his eyes the others had never seen before. Laying his large hand on top of her head, he spoke in a gentle tone. "I'm not going to let them hurt you, little black-eyed girl. That's a promise."

"They say history repeats itself," Jarrell observed.

"What do you mean?" asked Rosa.

"Almost exactly forty-one years ago, Colonel William Travis, Davy Crockett, Jim Bowie, and the brave men with them were attacked on this very spot."

A gasp escaped Armand Tejada's lips. Eyes wide, he said, "You are right, Stu! It was March sixth, eighteen thirty-six!"

"At *dawn*," added Jarrell. "That's when Santa Anna's troops stormed this place and wiped out that little handful of men who had fought so gallantly to establish Texas as a free republic."

Wolf Bixler's rough features took on a bold look of determination. He said jaggedly, "Get to your stations!"

Rosa sent Josefina into the baptistery room, and then Wolf's small army took their guns and scattered in four directions, assuming that Vomero would surround the big stone building on all four sides with his superior numbers. Wolf took the front corner room and peered through the flyspecked window facing the convent. As he watched the Mexicans standing out there, guns ready, he suddenly realized that some were out of his view. He could not see the covered wagon from this window. Dashing to the back corner room where Jarrell waited, Wolf pointed out to him that the irregular shape of the building created a blind spot that could not be seen from either end without sticking their heads all the way out the windows.

Counting the Mexicans he could see from Jarrell's window, and adding them to the ones he had just seen from his own, Wolf was sure the whole bunch was still gathered between the chapel and the convent. They had not surrounded the building.

"When they start shootin'," said Wolf, "we need to pin them in that blind spot, near the wagon, and then hit them from the roof. They will have nowhere to go since the doors and windows of that other building are sealed up."

"There aren't enough of us," argued the marshal.

"There would be if I could get that machine gun up on that flat roof," said Wolf. "There's a trapdoor in the ceiling of an alcove just off the nave at the back of the chapel. It has to lead to the roof. Has a ladder leadin' to it. With the boy turnin' the crank, I could hold the Gatling in both hands and spray the whole area with lead. If you and the girl could shoot at them from the windows at both ends on this side, we can keep them penned in and cut them down."

"Sounds feasible," agreed Jarrell. "But that Gatling must weigh more than two hundred pounds. I know you carried it in here from the wagon . . . but up a ladder?"

"I can do it," Wolf assured him. "Go bring those two in here. Our five minutes is up."

As Jarrell hastened across the nave to get Rosa and Armand and tell them the new plan, Wolf moved toward the big machine gun.

Suddenly he heard hoofbeats out in the courtyard. Someone was riding in. Rushing to the front corner of the room, Wolf peered through the window and saw two mounted men wearing badges questioning the Mexicans.

Stuart Jarrell shouldered in beside Wolf, with Rosa and Armand at his heels. "What's going on?" asked the marshal, brushing cobwebs from the window frame.

"Looks like Vomero's got trouble with the law," commented Wolf.

Jarrell instantly recognized Sheriff Ted Traxler, the man he had rescued from the four roughnecks in San Antonio. The other man, he assumed, must be his deputy. Traxler was asking about the four dead Mexicans in front of the chapel.

Vomero's voice became loud and belligerent as he walked into view saying, "You had best ride away and forget you saw any of this, Sheriff!"

"Vomero sure is mean looking." Armand spoke quietly, peering through a low corner of the window.

"Like a teased snake," Jarrell dryly remarked.

Ted Traxler bristled at Vomero's harsh words. "What do you mean, forget it?" he snapped. "There are four dead men lying there, and I'm the law in this town. Now I want some answers!"

"You do as I told you, Sheriff!" Vomero snarled.

The deputy stiffened and went for his gun.

"No!" Traxler said, attempting to stop the deputy's foolish move.

It was too late. Guns roared, and the two lawmen peeled out of their saddles, riddled with bullets.

"We'd better get ready," Wolf breathed, turning away. "Stu, fill the girl in on what we're doing. You two have got to keep them boxed in. Boy, you come with me."

While Jarrell explained the strategy to Rosa, Wolf led Armand to where the Gatling gun sat on the floor of the nave. Pointing to the circular metal magazines that were stacked nearby, he said, "Grab one of those. We're goin' up on the roof."

Each magazine held a hundred rounds of .58 caliber cartridges, and one was already in position on the gun. Wolf figured that two hundred rounds should be sufficient.

Armand had the heavy magazine in his hands when he turned around to see the six-foot-six-inch man hoist the two-hundred-fifty-pound Gatling gun onto his shoulder. "You're going to turn the crank for me, boy," said Wolf. "Okay?"

"Yes!" exclaimed Armand, honored to be given such an important job.

"Do you think you can carry that magazine up a ladder?" Wolf asked him.

"Of course," answered the dark-skinned youth. Lifting the cartridge-filled magazine to his shoulder, simulating Wolf's stance, he said, "I will follow you."

As Wolf wheeled, he saw Josefina peeking out the door of the baptistery room. Huskily, he said, "You stay in there, little black-eyed girl. I don't want a stray bullet findin' you."

The door immediately shut.

Wolf and Armand were heading for the trapdoor

when Aldo Vomero's sharp voice penetrated the chapel wall. "Your time is up, Bixler!"

Wolf balanced the big death machine on his right shoulder, steadying it with his right hand while adjusting the ladder under the trapdoor with his left. He was starting up the ladder when Vomero's army cut loose with their rifles.

Bullets whanged and chewed into the chapel's side door and into the windows of the rooms where Jarrell and Rosa waited.

Glass shattered at Rosa's window as bullets peppered the opposite wall. When the volley had ended, she swung the rifle in her hands to the open window frame and aimed at a nearby guerrilla. The rifle bucked against her shoulder, and the man collapsed. Before the men close by him could react, she worked the lever and nipped another one in the arm.

Rosa pulled back just in time to escape a shower of lead that assaulted the window.

Down the same side of the chapel at the other end, Stuart Jarrell, grinding broken glass under his boots, fired three times, bringing down the man Rosa had shot in the arm. A hail of lead chewed the wall as he ducked for cover.

Realizing their vulnerability, the Mexicans pulled in closer to the center, where they found safety in the blind spot.

Straining his every muscle, Wolf Bixler slid the heavy machine gun onto the chapel roof and then climbed through the square opening into the orange light of the rising sun. The light wind plucked at the dark locks on his hatless head. Bending low, he reached back and steadied Armand, as the boy reached the flat surface of the roof. They could hear the gunfire down below.

Wolf caught his breath and then said, "Now, boy, I'm going to carry the gun over to the side where Vomero is."

Armand nodded, ready for his instructions.

Wolf eyed the two-foot wall that extended around the odd-shaped perimeter of the roof. "I'll have to point the muzzles over that short wall," he said. "When I say go, you turn the crank till I tell you to stop. Got it?"

"Sí," replied Armand, his eyes showing some apprehension.

At that instant, the firing down below stopped, and Wolf lifted the Gatling, bracing it against his right hip. Armand followed, laying the spare magazine down as they neared the edge. Bending over to avoid being seen from below, he hastily moved up to the right side of the gun, touching the handle of the crank with his fingertips.

Aldo Vomero's voice lifted out of the silence. "Bixler! I am not fool enough to try to come through a door when you have the Gatling gun in there! Do not be stupid! We have you trapped. All we have to do is wait. Sooner or later you will need food and water. If you insist on this foolishness, you will all die!"

Peering over the edge of the roof, Wolf could see two guerrillas lying dead. The others were huddled near the covered wagon, where they could not be seen from the windows where Rosa and Jarrell waited. Vomero knew he could rush the windows and take out those who manned them, but he did not want to lose the men it would cost to do it. He would try other measures.

"All I want is the Gatling, Bixler!" Vomero shouted. "Do you hear me? I want my machine gun! Just let me have it, and we will go away. I promise!"

Inching the tip of the shiny tubular casing over the edge, Wolf pointed the deadly muzzles into the cluster of Mexican guerrillas. Standing with knees bent, holding the Gatling steady, he said, "Go, boy!"

With a firm grip on the crank, Armand threw his shoulder into it.

One Mexican looked up and saw the forms on the roof just as the gun broke loose. The man started to speak, but never got a word out.

The deep-throated voice of the Gatling echoed and reverberated across the compound of the Alamo. The guerrillas scattered as Wolf sprayed the area. Dust puffs rose by the dozens as .58 caliber slugs bit into the ground.

Aldo Vomero flattened himself against the wall of the chapel, where the bullets could not reach, shouting for his men to do the same. In panic, one of them ran to escape the trap they were in, and he went down under the hail of hot lead.

Wolf hollered at Armand to stop, and the death machine went silent. Thick wisps of smoke lifted from the hot muzzles.

Aldo Vomero, his back to the chapel wall, looked straight up. The only thing exposed over the edge of the roof was the smoking tip of the Gatling. The guerrilla leader knew it was useless to shoot at it. He made a quick count. There were three men flattened against the wall with him. Two others were taking refuge under the covered wagon. The remaining two sprawled lifelessly in the dust.

Turning to two men who stood against the wall at his right, Vomero whispered, "Franco, Manuel . . . you have got to crawl under the window and get to the back of the building. You must find a way to get on the roof. The man firing the Gatling must be stopped. Kill him!"

To give his two men cover, Vomero fired his pistol at the edge of Stuart Jarrell's window while they hastened underneath.

On the roof, Wolf set the Gatling down. Resting his arms, he said to Armand, "I've got to drive them away from the wall. I'm going to empty both revolvers over the edge, shootin' straight down. You be ready when I pick up the Gatling. We'll spray them."

"Be careful, Wolf," warned Armand. "You will have to expose yourself to do that. They can return fire from down there."

Pulling his lips tight, Wolf drew both Colts. Dropping to his knees, he plunged head, shoulders, and guns over the edge and blasted away, shooting straight down the walls.

Vomero and the one man remaining with him against the wall unleashed their guns up at Wolf, and the big man pulled back as bullets howled and whined, chipping stone from the roof's edge.

Meanwhile, the two guerrillas under the covered

wagon had concluded that their only hope was to push the wagon toward the front gate of the compound. They would stay underneath for protection, moving it while crawling on their knees. The tail end of the wagon was facing the courtyard, so they would move it backward in that direction. One man would guide it by crawling along with his hands on the front axle.

When Aldo Vomero saw the wagon begin to move, he shouted, "Stop, you fools!"

On the roof, Wolf Bixler heard Vomero's voice and then the sound of the wagon wheels squeaking. Within a few seconds the canvas top came into view as the Mexicans moved it toward the street, the long tongue dragging.

Wolf picked up the Gatling and said, "Okay, boy, get ready."

Armand drew close as the big man moved to the roof's edge and aimed the ten muzzles at the covered wagon.

Suddenly, from below, Rosa saw the wagon come in line with her window. She saw what was happening and opened fire, shooting through the spokes of the slow-turning wheels.

Wolf hollered, "Go!"

Armand turned the crank vigorously. The big gun boomed, spitting fire. Bullets whipped through the canvas, shredding it and tearing through the floor of the bed. The guerrillas were screaming, being hit from both levels.

Aldo Vomero and the guerrilla with him started to scrape along the wall, moving toward the rear of the chapel. Stuart Jarrell heard Rosa open fire and stuck his head out the window to see what she was shooting at. He saw instead Vomero and his cohort inching their way in his direction. Swinging his revolver out the window, he shot the man closest to him and then quickly withdrew from the window.

As the man in front of him flopped to the ground, Vomero fired at Jarrell, but the marshal had drawn back in the nick of time. Then Jarrell stuck his hand out the window, aimed the revolver blindly, and fired.

The slug tore into Vomero's right shoulder, and the gun slipped from his hand as he slid down the wall to a sitting position. Grimacing in pain, he clutched his shoulder with his left hand.

Jarrell risked a look out the window and saw that the wounded guerrilla leader was out of commission. He ran his gaze over the bodies strewn across the area between the chapel and the convent. There was no movement. The Gatling on the roof was still ripping at the covered wagon. Bolting from the room, Jarrell headed toward Rosa.

While Armand turned the crank and Wolf raked the wagon below, Franco and Manuel were bellying over the edge of the roof at the back of the chapel building.

Wolf hollered for Armand to stop cranking and then turned around, just as the two Mexicans were taking aim at himself and the boy.

In a split second of instinctive reflex, Wolf swung a huge arm and knocked Armand rolling. Manuel's shot cut air where Armand had been standing, but Franco's bullet hit Wolf in the chest.

The big man began losing his grip on the heavy gun. He went to his knees, grasping the Gatling. The two Mexicans ignored Armand, firing their guns at Wolf.

He felt the angry slugs tearing into his body as he rested the Gatling's base on the roof and turned the crank. The big machine gun belched fire, and Franco and Manuel died as the smoking .58 caliber bullets tore through their chests.

Armand went to Wolf, who was balancing on his knees, clinging to the Gatling. "Wolf!" he exclaimed. "You saved my life!" Then he gasped as he saw the bullet holes in Bixler's shoulders and chest. "Wolf, you're hit bad!"

The big man drew a ragged breath and said, "Boy, it's quiet down there on the ground. Go take a look and tell me if you can see Vomero. Be real careful now."

Armand dashed to the edge of the roof and eased his head out slowly. He saw Vomero. Quickly he returned and said, "He is down there, Wolf, near Stuart's window, sitting on the ground with his back against the wall. His shoulder is bleeding. There are many other dead guerrillas."

"You mean he's leaning against the wall of *this* building?" asked the mortally wounded man.

"Sí. Near the back window."

Summoning strength from somewhere deep within, Wolf Bixler gritted his teeth and hoisted up the big machine gun, cradling it in his arms. With pained effort, he rose to his feet. "Show me just where Vomero's sittin', boy," he murmured.

Armand ran to the spot at the roof's edge directly above Aldo Vomero. Wolf staggered toward the boy, carrying the two-hundred-fifty-pound gun.

Suddenly Armand saw Stuart Jarrell moving among the corpses below, a revolver in each hand. Seeing the youth appear, the marshal called to him, "Get down, kid! There are still two guerrillas unaccounted for. Vomero won't tell me where they are."

"They are up here on the roof," Armand told him. "Wolf killed them! But he is—"

"Move aside, boy," Wolf gasped, setting the Gatling on the two-foot-high wall at the roof's edge.

Jarrell watched from the ground as the big gun teetered on the edge above Vomero's head. He could see the splotches of blood on Wolf's shirt.

Looking down at the Mexican, Wolf shouted with effort, "Hey, Vomero!"

Vomero tilted his head back and lifted his gaze upward to see the huge dark object rocking precariously above him.

"Seems I heard you say you wanted your Gatling gun, Vomero," Wolf grunted, his dark eyes gleaming with venomous pleasure. "Well, here it is!"

Wolf let the big gun tilt over the edge and fall.

Just before the impact, Stuart Jarrell turned his head, not wanting to see the Mexican be crushed by the falling weight.

"Stu!" called Armand.

Jarrell looked up to the rooftop and saw Wolf Bixler stagger, reel, and collapse.

Chapter Eighteen

Stuart Jarrell helped Rosa and Josefina up the ladder to the rooftop, where they gathered with Armand beside the mortally wounded Wolf Bixler. Looking down at the big man, Rosa could see at once why Jarrell had decided not to try to move him but instead had summoned her and Josefina to the roof.

Josefina's brow was furrowed. Looking up at the worried face of her aunt, she said, "Rosa, will Uncle Wolf be all right?"

Rosa could not answer because her throat had constricted with emotion. She dropped to her knees, watching the five bullet holes bubble with blood at every heave of Wolf's thick chest.

Josefina brushed close to her aunt's shoulder, her little face shadowed with sorrow. She knew the answer to her question.

Jarrell and Armand knelt down on the other side of the dying man.

Wolf looked up at the four faces with languid eyes. The pallor of death was on his features. His voice was weak, but the words came in a deep tone. "Any of you . . . get hit?"

"No," answered Armand, smiling at his idol, "but if you had not pushed me down, I would be dead."

Rolling his smoky eyes to Stuart Jarrell, Wolf asked, "Did we get . . . all of them?"

"Yes." Jarrell nodded, thinking of the terror in Aldo

Vomero's eyes that last split second before the Gatling gun crushed his skull. "They're all dead."

Swallowing hard, the big man sucked in a painful breath and then mumbled, "Guess that Waco . . . prison will have to get . . . along without me."

A faint smile curved Jarrell's lips. "After what we've been through together," he said softly, "I probably would have let you sock me on the head and run away, anyhow."

Shedding tears, little Josefina dropped to her knees and planted a kiss on Wolf Bixler's craggy cheek. Looking at him tenderly, she said, "I love you, Uncle Wolf. You really are my Uncle Wolf, aren't you?"

Rosa choked back a hot lump in her throat when she saw tears in the burly man's eyes.

"Yes," he breathed out raggedly. "I really am . . . your Uncle Wolf."

Josefina smiled, wiping tears from her cheeks with the back of her hand.

Setting his glazed eyes on Jarrell and then rolling them to Rosa, Wolf said, "You two make a happy . . . life together."

The couple nodded wordlessly, fighting their own tears.

Looking at Armand, Wolf coughed and said, "You're a . . . real fightin' man, boy. Wish . . . wish we could have been partners."

Pride welled up within Armand Tejada, and he bit down on his quivering lip.

The massive man turned his attention back to Josefina, who still hovered over him. "Little black-eyed girl . . ."

"Yes, Uncle Wolf?" came the tiny, sorrow-filled voice.

With effort, the dying man raised his huge arm and wrapped it around her. Pulling her down, he kissed her forehead and then cuddled her face against his muscular neck. In a choked half whisper, he said, "I love you, too."

With Josefina snug in his arm, Wolf closed his eyes. Jarrell, Rosa, and Armand were still as they saw a smile form on his lips. Then the arm that held Josefina fell heavily, and his broad chest went still. Wolf Bixler died smiling.

As Rosa lifted the lifeless arm and pulled the child to her bosom, Jarrell sniffed and said, "He really did have a smile deep down inside."

"Yes." Rosa nodded, tears dripping from her chin. "But it took the love of a little black-eyed girl to put it on his face."

Epilogue

El Presidente Sebastian Lerdo de Tejada hastened out of Mexico City on November 20, 1876, and made his way to Acapulco. After a brief rest, he began a long voyage by sea to New York, where he spent the rest of his life in exile.

Tejada's flight at such a crucial time gave new life to Porfirio Díaz's revolt and demoralized the people's defense. Under the circumstances a great part of Tejada's army joined the Díaz faction, and the remainder gave up the fight. In vain the president of Mexico's supreme court, José Maria Iglesias, endeavored to cope with the situation, but in the face of a large rebel army, fully equipped and well trained, resistance was impossible.

On November 23, 1876, General Díaz entered Mexico City at the head of his army and proclaimed himself provisional president of the republic. Two months later a farcical congressional election was held, and the congress thus elected under the muzzles of the rebel guns declared Porfirio Díaz president of Mexico by the unanimous vote of the people on May 22, 1877.

STAGECOACH STATION 26:

TULSA

by Hank Mitchum

In September 1893, thousands of people gather in Tulsa, Oklahoma, for the last of the great land runs, hoping to claim a choice parcel of the Cherokee Strip, along the Oklahoma-Kansas border. Among those waiting for the gun's signal are Beth and Charlie Converse, a young couple from St. Louis, who see the land run as their last hope for happiness. Though Charlie's previous failures have eroded his self-esteem, his beautiful wife has remained faithful to him and his dream—even when Charlie has not.

Into their lives comes Jim Land, a deputy U.S. marshal assigned to capture the notorious Doolin gang. But Jim Land has a personal vendetta he wants settled at all costs—the arrest of the merciless killer Turk Freese, who escaped after being caught by Land and who is now said to be affiliated with Bill Doolin and his gang.

When Jim Land saves the Converses from losing their money to thieves, he makes an impression upon Beth that she does not soon forget—even after she and her ne'er-do-well husband have claimed their plot in the Cherokee Strip land run. But before the marshal can see her again, he must track down the villainous Turk Freese, and Beth must decide where her true allegiance lies—with her cheating husband or the handsome Jim Land.

Read TULSA, on sale November 1986 wherever Bantam paperbacks are sold.